VALERIA
NARBIKOVA

In the
Here and There

TRANSLATED BY MASHA GESSEN

ARDIS

Valeria Narbikova
In the Here and There
Copyright © 1999 by Valeria Narbikova

ISBN 0-87501-154-3

COVER PHOTOGRAPH: SVETLANA IVANOVA

ARDIS PUBLISHERS
24721 EL CAMINO CAPISTRANO
DANA POINT, CALIFORNIA 92629

In the Here
and There

SOMETHING ALWAYS PRECEDES that which follows. Here are three examples from an entirely different novel, with the first example illustrating the relativity of place, the second illustrating the permanence of time, and the third illustrating (see below).

Example one:

One day V.N. and I.K. arrive in Simferopol by plane late at night (at 2300 hours) but their destination is an entirely different place, 80 km from Simferopol. The only means of transportation to this other place is a taxi at a cost of 80 rubles, but, as this amount exceeds the cost of two plane tickets from Moscow to Simferopol, after solving the simple arithmetic problem in which the question is, Which is more expensive—by air or by land?—they turn down the taxi driver's offer not because of the awesome cost but because they are awed by the accessibility of travel by plane and the inaccessibility of travel by automobile. They board a trolley and, for the cost of 80 kop., proceed to Alushta so as to make a circle and reach the desired destination by sea. In Alushta, satisfied finally that no means of transportation operates at such a late hour, they decide to spend the night somewhere on the beach. But the beach, which is divided into segments, is locked, and with the intention of lying down somewhere in the bushes, they depart for the woods that cover the mountain. The mountain is in the very center of the town; rather, the town is situated on the mountain. Having put some distance between themselves and the center of town, they discover a very dark and discreet part of warm earth covered with warm pine needles and soft cypress branches. They sit down and when their eyes get a little bit used to the darkness, they can see that there is a road a bit below them, about 50 meters away, and that a bit above them, there is some sort of structure (a building?). To be precise, a building and yet not. In the darkness, it appears to be of approximately three stories or possibly four but at the same time it is unfinished and seemingly uninhabited, not fenced off but somehow official in appearance, possibly a tailor shop or a post office, though nothing indicates that either is the case. It is definitely not a hotel or a movie theater but a building of unknown function. But because it is still dark, V.N and I.K. decide that when it gets light, they will determine with certainty what kind of building they are spending

7

the night by. They drink two bottles of Gyrdzhaani wine, which they have brought with them from Moscow, and fall asleep, beautifully, right on the ground. When they wake up at 6 o'clock in the morning, they see this "building" in the soft gray light of a southern morning, but they are still unable to determine what kind of building it is. As they pack their bags and collect pieces of paper and empty bottles (their trash), they exchange theories about this building, though none of these theories satisfies them.

"It's not a post office."

"Nah."

"It's not finished."

"Why not? It's got glass, and that over there looks like a curtain."

"It looks somehow unfinished."

"A creepy kind of place—what did you do with my bag?"

"I slept on it—it's kind of scary."

"Money fell out of your pants pockets—a weird kind of place."

"Let's get out of here fast."

Wrapping up quickly, they practically roll off the mountain, beating it from the inexplicable place with the inexplicable building. In the end, it is inexplicable what kind of place this was, unrecognizable not only in the dark but in the light as well.

Example two:

As they await the arrival of their friends bringing beer, V.N. and I.K. look longingly at the pointy cape that cuts into the sea somewhat more abruptly than the rest of the shapes, which are elliptically semicircular. From their location at one point, they are looking at another point, located at a distance of 5 km from them; they are looking from Novy Svet to Sudak, and from this point, being absolutely real in Novy Svet, they can distinguish absolutely no people in Sudak, and have only their knowledge that the concave shore and the pointy cape over there constitute Sudak. After losing all hope that their friends will ever return with the beer, and after holding a lengthy discussion on the topic that it would be faster to go themselves, they find themselves, albeit not too soon, in Sudak, in the very point they observed as but a point from Novy Svet. But now Novy Svet, the place where they were not too long ago, appears to them to be a point. It is difficult to say in which point they are really real, since only about six hours elapse between Novy Svet and Sudak. But if we ignore

8

that time, which is merely a grain in the sand of time, merely a drop in the ocean—the ocean of time—then it turns out they are really real in two points at the same time.

Example three:

A person (a relative?) attempts to write the life story of an author on the basis of a novel that has accidentally come into his possession. Details that appear to be entirely biographical horrify him, and he imagines the rest of the author's life by filling in these details from the book. When the author learns of this, he is horrified by the way in which people in general (relatives?) read books. The author becomes very agitated and refuses to acknowledge that the details were entirely autobiographical, but this begs the question of why the author took such care to camouflage everything so carefully in his novel if those details were not autobiographical...

PART ONE

If it's a thought, then what kind of thought is it? They had covered kilometers walking from one room to the other.

"You just don't give a damn about anything," the older sister said to the younger sister.

"About what?"

"About anything."

With every word they moved farther apart.

"What did I ever do to you?" said the younger sister and sat down.

"You didn't do anything to me," answered Yezdandukta.

"Then tell me, what did I do?"

"I'll tell you. You're intolerable, Petia, and I only tolerate you because you are my sister."

"I know, it's not like you'd want to marry me," said Petrarka. "But we are related."

Yezdandukta didn't answer this. She stuffed herself into a sweater, pulled on a pair of shoes, and when she was already standing in the doorway, she said, "So this is how you treat relatives?"

"Tell me, what did I do that was so bad?" said Petia.

And as the door was shut on this question, the question was left stuck in the door.

It's a city fall like... if it's fall, then what kind of fall is it? The *beautiful* sun, moving across a *luxuriously blue* sky, shone its rays straight down onto dirt that had been uncovered: potholes, boards, pieces of paper swollen from rain. And the wind, going over the garbage dumpsters in a *slight* gust, showered the pavement with watermelon rinds, fruit pits and apple cores—the *generous* gifts of fall. It is not like winter, when garbage, frozen into the ground and covered with a *thin layer of snow,* weakly sprouts *early* growth, but precisely fall, which is so *bountiful.* And the day is pumped full of sounds, each of which is a *triumph* of conscious *human* activity: the sounds of trolleys and trams, which *celebrate* the *power* of *humankind,* that of which *humans* are capable on this *morning* that is both *beautiful* and *sunny* at the end of the twentieth century.

Petia had fallen in love with Boris. She knew that she loved him and only him, and that the only thing she knew was that she loved him.

Boris was late. They were supposed to meet at the front of the platform, by the first car of the train, and the train was already at the platform, but it had arrived in the opposite direction and the first car was at the rear of the platform, and now Petia didn't know why Boris wasn't there or where he was and whether she should remain at the front of the platform or go to the first car at the other end of the platform. All this was so terrible that Anna Karenina should immediately have jumped in front of the train she was taking to see Vronsky when she was late to see him—and not only should she have jumped, but Vronsky's mother, who was travelling with her, should have jumped as well, so Anna would not have to be tortured by her throughout the entire novel, so Vronsky would be left without Anna from the very beginning and could grieve for her through the entire novel and not just in the last chapter. Boris found Petia in the middle of the platform, where she stood the way she stood: like a shadow. And as soon as he saw her, he heard: "Don't go!"

"I'll come back soon," he said. "In three days."

and a minute later she said, "Don't go!" And he said: "I'll come right back."

and right away she said, "Don't go!"

And while she was trying to talk him out of leaving, the train left and Boris stayed. The train left without Boris, it left absolutely empty, and jumping in front of it would have been pointless, since it couldn't have killed anyone because it was light as a feather. But Boris was left with a heavy heart after the train left so lightly and so quickly.

Petia had already loved Boris an eternity, which had rushed by in the month they had known each other. She needed to see him every day, several times a day. Her eyes were empty from happiness, and there was not a thought in her head except for thoughts of Boris.

What impressed her about Boris was what had not impressed her at all at first. At first she had not been impressed at all by his appearance, but later any man who resembled Boris the least bit became worthy of her attention, especially since Boris's appearance was fairly typical among men: he had straight hair, a straight nose, light eyes and light hair. He looked young for forty but old for thirty. In general, his appearance was such that any man's appearance could have been reduced to Boris's appearance. At first she had not been impressed at all by his work. If Boris's appearance was typical, then his work was absolutely atypical: he didn't go to work. What he had the opportunity to make at home he wouldn't have had the opportunity to make at work; at home he made sculptures that rang, shone, walked, sat, and one of which had a title, "The Eyes Are the Mirror of the Soul," featuring a perfectly ordinary pair of doll's eyes set in a perfectly ordinary mirror, and this was precisely the work that impressed her in a way it had not impressed her at first. Even her first night with Boris, which ended in the morning, seemed entirely unimpressive to Petia during the day, and in the evening she didn't call Boris. But when her head filled with the ways in which she had not been impressed with Boris, she fell in love with him head over heels.

As for the sculptures that Boris made, they would have sold out all over the world as well as at the store World of Art, but Boris never traveled anywhere, unlike Gogol, who traveled, as did Turgenev and Dostoyevsky; like Pushkin, he didn't travel except to the country and to the Caucasus, but never beyond Mikhailovskoye or Bakhchisarai. Right away, Petia fell in love with this one temple, the model of which Boris didn't show her right away but only after he fell in love with her himself. From the outside this temple looked like a regular nine-story tower, a white concrete-block matchbox, not a bit different from all the other nine-story towers in Moscow; but inside it embodied the outside of the Kolomensky Temple: in other words, when a person ended up inside this concrete-block matchbox, what appeared before his eyes was a concave Kolomensky Temple: every protrusion of the Kolomensky Temple became a concavity of the Boris Temple, and under the roof of the nine-story tower was a concave dome, which was blue with gold stars.

After Boris didn't leave by train, he left almost immediately by foot; he and Petia parted at the railroad station to meet again tomorrow at Petia's house, after her sister left.

Yezdandukta could not forgive Petia for the Korean airliner incident, as if Petia had shot it down. It so happened that a month before Petia met Boris the Korean airliner was shot down and Petia and her friends pretended to be the airliner, which wore dark "spy" glasses on its nose. But then the "airliner" would demonstratively remove the spy glasses and shyly don a pair of regular children's prescription glasses, and at that point everyone else would start firing at those glasses, and the glasses would break, so the "airliner" couldn't see anything and would start trip-ping over various objects—shelves, chairs, tables—and then, with some difficulty, would make its way to the bathroom, and as soon as the door closed behind it, it would noisily fall into the toilet, and then it would get quiet so everyone could hear the peaceful murmur of water in the toilet.

"Retards," said Yezdandukta. "This will get you nowhere fast."

"Where?" asked Petia.

"Why are you asking me a question I already answered?" And after a brief silence, she answered again: "Nowhere."

There was nothing repellent about Yezdandukta's face; it was attractive, even. It attracted so that it could repel. It attracted the way the face of a little animal that's been artificially bred by human beings attracts through its anomaly: a small nose becomes smaller and smaller in the process of breeding, until it disappears entirely, and eyes become bigger and bigger, and the ears thin-ner, and the neck thicker. Plus, Yezdandukta applied her makeup in an unfortunate manner that made everything that was already small seem even smaller and everything that was already large seem even larger.

...if it's words, then what kind of words are they? The kind that would reach Yezdandukta before Boris called; the kind that would make her leave right away, without saying one rude thing to Petia.

As if for spite, Yezdandukta was getting ready as if she were going to a ball: first she put on one skirt and one blouse, then she put on a different skirt and a different blouse to go with it. She drank tea and then went back to finish it. Along with her unfin-ished tea she finished her uneaten sandwich. When Petia jumped to the phone when Yezdandukta had already picked up the re-ceiver, when Petia said "It's for me" when Yezdandukta had al-ready hung up saying "They hung up," Petia sat down by the phone in total despair the reason for which was Yezdandukta. As the reason, she was pacing back and forth for no reason and hurt-ing Petia with this unreasonable pacing. Having lost hope that she would ever depart, Petia thought only of the hope that she would depart. The reason for Petia's pain was Yezdandukta, who couldn't depart, and the consequence of Petia's pain was Boris, who couldn't arrive. In the end the cause and the effect got so confused that Boris, who couldn't arrive, became the cause of her pain, and Yezdandukta, who couldn't depart, became the effect of this pain, and the fact that Raskolnikov killed the old lady was the cause,[1] and the fact that he was condemned to hard labor was the effect, and the killing was the crime and the hard labor was the punishment, but it would be better if he had labored first and then killed the old lady, and it would be better if the Decembrists[2] had been exiled first and then had come out onto Senate Square, and the scariest thing was when the effect traded places with the cause, and more than anything else Petia was afraid that first Boris wouldn't arrive and then Yezdandukta would depart, that first Napoleon would be sent to St. Helena and then he would conquer the world.

"Nowhere," said Petia when Yezdandukta asked her where she was going today.

"Just like this," she answered when Yezdandukta said, "Are you going to walk around all day looking like that?"

And after Yezdandukta said nothing else and Petia said nothing else back, Yezdandukta left almost immediately, and almost immediately there was a call from Boris.

"Well?"

"Where are you?"

"Is your house across from the post office?"

"Are you by the post office?"

Petia named the floor and the apartment number. And as soon as she opened the door for him and as soon as she had had time enough to close the door and as soon as they hugged, they didn't stop hugging, all they did was hug something awful and kiss right there by the door next to the coat rack. "Take your coat off already." "Take yours off." Boris kept his coat on, while Petia was wearing a nightgown in which she was as hot as though she were wearing a coat, and in the rear of the "coat" she had a giant hole, and when she stuck her face in a coat that was hanging on the rack, Boris unbuttoned his coat while Petia kept wearing her holey "coat," and then he used the hole in her gown, this absolutely obvious hole in the plane, to reach space, he used a vacuum to reach a depth.

"Tell you later," he said when she asked, "What are you doing?" because he had sighed in a way that sounded like he couldn't breathe.

"Tell me now."

"Later."

And later, when they were drinking wine and Boris was looking around her room, which he was wild about right away, with the just-written poems pinned to the wallpaper still drying and with its cast-metal butterfly that looked real from afar because it even had metal antennae, Petia asked: "What did you want to tell me when you said you'd tell me later?"

"I'll tell you later."

"When?"

And when they left the building together to avoid being caught by the sister, Boris saw a hole in the fence that led to the opening of a concrete pipe, and when Petia and Boris climbed through the hole in the fence they ended up inside the pipe, when they traversed the hole in the plane, they ended up in the deep darkness of space, they reached a depth through a vacuum, together they ended up inside Petia in the hallway by the coat rack, and now they were together and kissing inside Petia, bending their necks to fit in the pipe.

"Got it," said she.

"Cool," said he. And they did it again: they climbed through the hole in the fence into the pipe.

"You think the construction workers know about this?" asked Petia.

"About your holey gown?"

"Now it seems to me like everyone knows about it, like you fucked me publicly through the hole in the fence."

If it's the height of happiness, then what's higher? the shortest route to happiness starts with happiness itself. It's not the kind of long route they took in the last century, when they began with a light gust of wind and ended with a storm; this begins with a storm and ends with a storm. If Petia's love had begun in the nineteenth century, then it would just be reaching its climax at the end of the twentieth century, because in the last century Boris would just have had time to notice, first, how *silky* Petia's eyelashes are and how *radiant* her skin is, and Boris would be moving toward his happiness without rushing, in total harmony with nature, and some moonlit night or during a thunderstorm or at noon, he and Petia wouldn't let their happiness get away and their happiness wouldn't let them get away. Boris was hugging his girl who was no longer a maiden, and the fact that he wasn't her first and the fact that she wasn't his first, and what came first was that second, she was his first love and that first, he was her first love, and the fact that during her first year of college

18

she had her first man, who was a second-year student for whom she was his first—that was all secondary.

Petia fell asleep thinking of Boris, and when she woke up because she was thinking of Boris, she couldn't fall asleep for thinking of Boris. The earliest thought about Boris got her out of bed, and she didn't even think of thinking other thoughts. She valued her thought about Boris so much that the only thing more valuable was Boris's thought about Petia. If sex as a physical characteristic in the nineteenth century became sex as a concept in the twentieth century, then Boris, as a person in the last century, became, in the present century, in the transition from past to present, the concept of love, because before Boris Petia had no concept of love. Petia thought Boris, and for her he became not merely a proper name—Boris—he became the proper name for her love and her own proper name, and not one language, not even the "great and mighty" Russian,[3] had a name for it, only the dead Latin language, which no one spoke, could unite Petia and Boris into one whole and name this whole properly: *borisus*.

...if it's a life, then what's it like? it could be lived in such a way that wasn't the way of—like it's long but not in such a way as to always be ahead of you.

Boris's home was his castle, and in his castle Boris was at home. It had a piece of metal garden fence, the Kolomensky Temple in a box, a tree stump—all this luxury. And the model of "the temple from inside" was as tall as a person, and when Petia and Boris entered the inside of the temple, their heads ended up right in the dome, and the dome was close enough to kiss and all the stars were close enough to kiss and Petia kissed one of the stars. There is no feeling that cannot be expressed through words, but there are no words that can express the feeling and the kiss that has left its imprint on the lips and on the plaster when the plaster carries the imprint of lips the way the sky carries the imprint of a pink cloud washed out by the wind the way plaster carries the imprint of pink lipstick washed out by the rain. Petia showed Boris how red her throat was; it was painful for her to swallow after the kiss. Even feelings as hot as theirs were powerless here, where only warm beer could make the throat better, warm beer being more powerful than the hottest of feelings. Petia lay down, and Boris went to warm up the beer. She drank a glass and then another glass, and the third glass affected her in such a way that when Boris touched his lips, ice-cold from ice-

19

cold beer, to her lips, warm from warm beer, because of the colossal difference in temperature Petia and Boris tried another remedy, namely that she took a mouthful of water, except it wasn't water, and when he said "Spit it out if you can't swallow," she couldn't answer right away because she had her mouth full and only after she swallowed did she answer, "I can."

As they were tending to themselves at this rate, time didn't stand still either, and the speed of this treatment speeded up time to such a degree that when they looked out onto the street they saw that where it had been light it had become dark while conversely, under the street lights it had become light.

"What are you going to tell your sister?" asked Boris.

"I was at a birthday party," Petia replied to Yezdandukta when she showed up at home in the morning.

Between Boris's question and Petia's answer stretched a night so happy and truthful that Petia couldn't be truthful with Yezdandukta because this truth would not have brought happiness.

"I couldn't," Petia replied to Yezdandukta's reproachful "Couldn't you have called?"

"I did," said Petia when Yezdandukta said, "Did you even think of me?"

Petia did think that she would never tell her sister the truth about Boris because Yezdandukta would think it wasn't true and it was better to have Yezdandukta thinking that what isn't true isn't true than to have her thinking that what is true isn't true, which would truly be worse.

And when it was morning, it was like a morning that can only happen on a day like this one was, when everything is like it is when everything else seems to be so unlike anything that it can change nothing.

When Petia didn't come home at night for the second time, Yezdandukta told her for the first time, "This is the last time." Petia left the house and was free to head in any direction. She headed not in the direction of the store, where her sister had asked her to go, but in the opposite direction. And when she was crossing the street, a trolley came to a stop so abruptly that it seemed to be functioning like a private car. Petia boarded the trolley, which had been hired by Kostroma and Dyl.

"We could have gotten a private car for three rubles," said Dyl.

"I like getting a trolley for three rubles," said Kostroma.

Kostroma handed three rubles to the boy driver, and the trolley headed for the grove, which was not a glassy grove or a wooden grove, but Silver Grove, possibly so named because of the pine trees, which could get to looking pretty silver in the winter or because of the silver creek or, possibly, because of the thirty silver points and the wooden house that had been given to Kostroma's grandfather by his place of service for his faithful service. He did as he was told. And what he was told, he did. He looked to the future so intently that his eyes had gotten glassy in the way the grove had not.

"Is your grandfather home?" asked Petia.

"He's on assignment," answered Kostroma.

"Dyl," said Petia, "I don't really feel like going with you. I was on my way to the store."

"What do you need at the store?" said Kostroma. "We've got everything at the place."

"You got bread?"

They were walking to Kostroma's grandfather's house—Kostroma's "grandhouse"—and talking about love.

"Kostroma, do you love your grandfather?" asked Dyl.

"What about you, Dyl—do you love your grandfather?"

"My grandfather was killed because of your grandfather."

"So was my grandmother," said Petia.

"Your grandmother would be old enough to be his grandfather's mother."

"That means it was like killing his mother—the worst sin of all."

"She wouldn't be old enough to be his mother, she'd be more like his sister."

"So it was like killing his sister."

"Even if it was like killing his daughter, that wouldn't change anything," said Kostroma. "I won't let you kill my grandfather."

"Who said anything about killing your grandfather?" asked Dyl. "Petia, do you have any plans to kill his grandfather?"

"Then why are we going there?" asked Petia.

"Did you think we were going there to kill his grandfather?" said Dyl. "We are going there to drink coffee."

"I won't let anyone kill my grandfather. He's like a baby now, just born into this world, still covered in his mother's blood."

"We're sick of you with your grandfather," said Dyl.

"Then leave me alone."

"Why are we going there?" asked Petia when they were already

21

in front of the "grandhouse."

"To get the suitcase," said Kostroma.

Climbing up to the second floor, which Kostroma was temporarily inhabiting, was like literally getting into the grandfather's head. "Show us the suitcase."

The decor of the room was quite extraordinary for an ordinary person. What was extraordinary was that perfectly ordinary chairs, couches and wardrobes were tagged like migratory birds, presumably to prevent the furniture from flying away. Petia sat down in a chair, which was tagged and numbered, and while Kostroma was crawling underneath the (tagged and numbered) couch, Petia looked out the (tagged and numbered) window, where she saw trees, which were tagged and numbered, and she saw fallen leaves that belonged to the trees that belonged to the house that belonged to Kostroma's grandfather, who did not own any of these belongings. The grandfather is going to live here until he dies, and when he dies another grandfather, exactly the same and slightly different, is going to live here. And in this space, which was permanent—with permanent furniture, walls and stories—the only thing that was temporary was the person, namely Kostroma's grandfather. This permanent decor, created once and for all, would allow only the kind of grandfather that was created in its own image. This was not a place where a person chose his decor but a place where the decor chose the person. And all the people the decor chose were mortal, while the decor itself was immortal. Even if this decor were buried, the numbered tags would remain and descendants could use them to recreate the chairs, wardrobes, etc.

Dyl just couldn't believe his eyes when Kostroma opened the suitcase. Kostroma opened it and then right away—bang!—closed it. And Dyl imagined that he'd imagined it. Petia didn't see that Kostroma opened the suitcase because she was looking out the window, and when she turned back toward the suitcase, it was already closed. It was an old-fashioned little suitcase with metal corners.

"Give me three rubles for the trolley," Petia said to Kostroma. "And I'll go." Kostroma stuck his hand in his pocket uncertainly, certain that he didn't have a three-ruble bill, and pulled out his handkerchief and his money along with it. And when he gave Petia the three-ruble bill and she turned to go, he opened the suitcase and when Petia looked, she saw that which she had only heard about before.

"Petrarka," said Kostroma. He said it loud and formal, but suddenly something happened to his voice and he said "Petrarka" again, but this time much softer. Kostroma picked up the suitcase like a jewelry box and presented it to Petia, who smiled, because it was stuffed with treasures, which appeal to all kinds of women—tsarinas, whores and virgins—but at the same time the contents of the suitcase could not be called treasures. That is, there was gold there and there were diamonds, but these were not decorations—that is, since they were in a jewelry box of sorts, they were decorations of sorts, but these were not the normal sort of decorations—rings, bracelets and pins; these were decorations of precisely the abnormal sort: medals.

"Who does all this belong to?" said Petia, and her question was barely audible, but Kostroma heard her and gave a barely audible answer: "You," but Petia did not hear him and said, more softly still, "Who?" but Kostroma did not hear her and said nothing else and it became so quiet that nothing was audible, that is, what became audible was that nothing could be heard. But when the metal jingled when Kostroma put down the jewelry box, absolutely everyone heard it. And Dyl asked Kostroma, absolutely calmly: "Where'd you get it?" Kostroma looked at him calmly and said, "Have you heard the joke about 'Where'd you get it, where'd you get it?'" Kostroma told the joke: a guy runs down the street with an ax in his hand, and another guy is running after him, screaming, "Where'd you get it?" The guy with the ax stops, bops him on the head with it, and keeps walking like nothing happened, walking and muttering, "Where'd I get it, where'd I get it? I bought it—duh."

"So that's what you are going to be muttering when they bop you," said Dyl.

"Why would they bop *me*?"

"What do you think—that they give out medals for this sort of thing?"

"Maybe they give out medals posthumously."

"Maybe they aren't real," asked Petia.

"What do you mean, not real?" Kostroma answered indignantly. "You think I would give forgeries to a beautiful girl?"

"Who's the beautiful girl?" Petia asked him.

"You. You are the beautiful girl."

And Dyl and Kostroma looked at Petia, whose face looked like a very feminine boy's face.

"You mean I'm not a beautiful girl?" asked Dyl.

And Petia and Kostroma looked at Dyl, whose face was so feminine that he looked more like a girl than like a boy, but for some reason, Petia's boyish face was attractive while Dyl's girlish face was repellent. The fact that Dyl was of the male sex and had many of the features of the opposite sex did not become him, while the fact that Petia was of the female sex and had features of the opposite sex became her so much that Kostroma became transfixed by her face, and her faced became flushed. Kostroma himself blushed frequently and this was especially striking because he was naturally white—white skin, white hair, white eyelashes and white eyebrows. And if he had been a girl and could apply makeup to his eyebrows and eyelashes, then they would have been noticeable, but since he was not a girl and could not apply makeup, what was noticeable was that they were barely noticeable.

"Are you trying to say that the whole suitcase belongs to Petrarka?" said Dyl.

"I said that already."

"Are you in love or something?"

"Is love a crime or something?"

"Wait," Petia stopped them. "I'm already in love."

Kostroma and Dyl looked at her as though she were guilty of a terrible crime.

"I'm in love. Is that a crime?"

"What do you mean, you are in love," said Kostroma. "With whom?"

Petia said nothing and stepped away from the suitcase.

"When did you fall in love? When they shot down the airliner, you weren't in love."

"Not yet."

"But that wasn't that long ago that it was shot down. When did you have time to fall in love?"

"Recently, almost right after it was shot down."

"It hasn't even been a month since it was shot down."

"No, it's been two months already," said Petia.

"Has it really been two months already?" asked Kostroma.

"Two months exactly," said Petia.

"So you fell in love right after the plane thing?"

"No, not right after. A month later."

"Who is he?" asked Kostroma.

24

"Who?" Petia was confused.

"Who?" Kostroma said again.

She said Boris—she said that it was he—that he and she—that without him she—and that when he is not, she—and that it can only be he—that she would have never—but he—and then he too—and she...

"Yeah, that's it," said Kostroma.

"What's 'it'?" asked Petia.

"The real thing," said Kostroma.

"The real thing deserves a Gold Star,"[4] said Dyl.

"The Admiral Ushakov Medal!"

"The St. George Cross!"

"They are all yours," said Kostroma and laid the medals at Petia's feet.

"Bring it out," he said to Dyl.

"Where is it?" asked Dyl.

"Under the couch, on the right."

Dyl reached under the couch, got out a bottle of cognac. "You've got glasses here too."

"Get out the glasses. Get out whatever is under there. There's some salami."

"Why don't you lock the stuff up under the couch?"

"What am I supposed to do—lock a hole?"

"A hole is exactly what you are supposed to lock."

They cut a few pieces, they filled the glasses, and they drank a shot each.

"To *it*," said Kostroma. "*It* is such a rarity these days. It is a great service to our people."

Five medals appeared on Petia's chest all at once.

"But really, love is such hard work, such hard work," said Dyl, "that you deserve the Labor Veteran medal. And you can be awarded the Gold Star," Dyl got talkative, addressing Kostroma. "Because you are in love."

"No, if only one person is in love, it doesn't count," said Kostroma. "Anybody can fall in love with somebody. Medals should only be awarded for the kind of feeling that affects two people," reasoned Kostroma. "Really, medals should be awarded not to people but to the feeling, and people should only serve as representatives of the feeling, the same way that medals are awarded for deeds and people serve as representatives of these deeds: if a particular speed is achieved, the Labor Veteran medal is awarded; if a certain time is achieved, the medal goes to the time."

"If they are for the feeling," said Petia, "then half the medals belong to Boris."

"Half belong to him," concurred Kostroma.

Nothing was left out—everything, including the unfinished bottle and the salami, went into the suitcase.

"You going to invite us to your wedding?" asked Dyl.

The taxi driver got them from the grove to the boulevard in a few minutes, and they gave him a few rubles when he stopped by the college where Petia and Kostroma were studying and Dyl used to study but dropped out but he could reenroll, while Petia and Kostroma could, conversely, drop out, and they crossed the boulevard toward the New Art Theater but the old one was worth two new ones put together, and Kostroma recited some poetry:

> A leg in the distance is the same leg,
> And eyes in the distance are the same eyes,
> And a star in the distance is still a star,
> But love in the distance is also love.

Dyl looked at Kostroma, who had no love, either in the present or in the distance, and who would do well to give up writing poetry.

"Recite something else," said Dyl.

Kostroma recited something else.

"Now sing something," said Petia.

So, with song and poetry, they arrived at Boris's building and looked at his apartment, which was on the first floor, a bit below the sidewalk even, but not in the basement. Petia looked down into his window, but he wasn't there.

"Should we wait?" asked Kostroma.

They hung out in the cold and Kostroma started reciting another poem, but Petia gave him the kind of look that made him stop and say that he hadn't finished it yet.

"If we had private property in this country," said Dyl, "we could go into a private café and warm up."

"You can't go into a state one?"

"No. It stinks in the state ones."

"What stinks?"

"The stuff people eat, that's what stinks."

26

"So it's the food that stinks."

"I like it when food smells instead of stinking."

"I wouldn't oppose everything becoming private property," said Petia.

"Who would?" said Dyl. "Everything should be private property, except for borders, which should belong to the state."

Petia thought a bit and said "We can go to my house," because she thought that her sister wasn't home. Since they had spent what they had to spend, they rode the Metro to Petia's house. And when Petia started to open the door, it was opened from the other side by Yezdandukta, and that wasn't bad, because she opened it and went back inside, but then Boris came from the other side. At the sight of Boris, Petia should have fainted, but the fact is that she didn't faint and that she kept standing and that she even took a step forward; she should have become speechless at the sight of Boris, and that she talked, and that she answered, and that she later asked—apparently, from the minute she saw Boris, she did not stop talking and only she thought that she was still and silent, because in reality she was walking and talking, and she thought that everyone was walking and talking, when in reality everyone was still and silent. Yezdandukta started asking, and Petia started explaining, but Yezdandukta couldn't understand anything and asked only for an explanation of where the medals came from, but Petia couldn't understand where Boris came from, and when Yezdandukta had her question met with Petia's answer—"From outer space"—she met Petia's question with Petia's answer: "From outer space." And Boris didn't understand that the medals were for love and kept slipping away from Dyl and Kostroma like a fish—one minute they had him and the next minute he was gone—but when he understood that they were for love, the medals began shining on his chest like fish scales. Petia never stopped laughing, because her love was endless and this was the end of love. Yezdandukta, who was absolutely white, said "Go away," which absolutely everyone heard. And Petia asked, "Who?" And she answered, "Everybody." And Petia and Boris, their medals jingling, headed for the door. Dyl and Kostroma headed for the door. And when everybody was going down the stairs together, Yezdandukta stuck her head out the door and said, "Boris, may I see you for a minute?" And Boris turned around and headed back for the door, and when the door shut after Boris, Petia wanted to go right back and open the door with her key, then she wanted to ring the doorbell, then to kick the door in with her foot, but when Kostroma said, "Come on, we'll wait downstairs," Petia followed Kostroma, and once downstairs, they started waiting. The first minute was like any other minute, but when five more minutes had passed and Petia started counting the minutes—"how long has it been?"—"Ten minutes"— and five more minutes had passed, Petia felt that it had already been an hour and she said she wasn't going to wait one more minute, and in exactly one minute they left, and in exactly one minute Boris came out. He stood in front of the door for a few minutes, then walked a full circle in a minute, then, after thinking a minute, he decided to go back in for a minute.

2

...WHEREAS THOSE WHO cannot have children can have an andy-baby, which is a small metal figurine that talks—or a different sort of andy-baby can be bred in an egg by taking the egg of a black chicken, replacing the egg white with sperm, plugging the egg with damp wax paper, and placing it under a pile of manure on the first day of a March moon; following a gestation period of thirty days a monster resembling a small person will appear; it will need to be fed earthworms and bird feed, and as long as it is alive, you will be happy.

"Do you at least know where we are?"

"Na-ah."

"This is a stadium."

"There is a big field, but there are no bleachers."

"Maybe there are bleachers on the other side and we are on the opposite side."

"Bleachers should be all around the perimeter of the field."

"And we are outside the perimeter of the bleachers."

"There's fog there."

"What kind of fog?"

"Nighttime fog, and the bleachers are in the fog."

"Then why are there stars?"

"The stars are in the sky; the fog is on the ground."

"Then what's in the sky?"

"Stars."

"And on the ground?"

"Bleachers."

"Is there a sip left?"

"Are you kidding?"

"Last night I had a dream about a woman who was really beautiful, with brown eyes and a red dress, and she said, 'When you are unhappy or when you are happy, think of me, and I'll come to you.' She had an eye in her forehead, in addition to two eyes in the usual places, and the eye in her forehead kept falling in toward the back of her head, then floating up like a bob, as though in some sort of little pipe that led to the back of the head, and then it would float up to the surface of the forehead," Petrarka related with feeling.

"Do you love him?" asked Kostroma.

"Boris is my love," replied Petia.

And Kostroma, anticipating that Petrarka was going to say something else about Boris, said something else: "See that, toward the sky? That's the barn where they keep the inventory."

And the insensitive Dyl said, "Anyone can tell Petrarka is in love."

Not only could they not see a barn from where they were sitting, they couldn't even see the bleachers, and they could only see the stadium in their imaginations.

And Petia became so emotional because of the things that were visible and invisible that she was lifted up almost half a meter off the ground, and when she landed—no, when she was still between the ground and the sky—during the moment of landing—no, when she had already stood up, she said, when she had sat down, "I love Boris."

She spoke and she could barely speak because she was overwhelmed by love, and she said nothing except that she loved Boris, and her speech was less like a speech than like a melody—tah-tah-tah-tah—some melody known to some bird, and the idea contained in this melody was so simple that one wanted to fall in love with some bird in the Caucasus that loved some branch in Esher and chirped, from the moment she greeted the sun with joy in the morning and until night: "I-love-Bo-ris." And if the bird's song were a ship signal or a trolley jingle or the sound of a car braking in the sky, this might have struck a listener, but there was nothing striking in the fact that a bird sings or a girl loves, in the very melody as idea or idea as melody. So she loves. So she sings.

"I'll never love anyone else. Never," said Petia. This new song was even more touching, and when she said, again, "Never," it started snowing, and closer to the sky, it was more like snow, and closer to the ground, it was more like raining, and it became very apparent that there are several levels between the ground and the sky. This was apparent from the point of view of a person, but it would have been good if it had been apparent from some other point of view as well.

Petia came home not too late, but later than the time at which Boris left and earlier than the time at which Yezdandukta went to sleep.

Yezdandukta was glowing like never before; that is, Petia had never before seen Yezdandukta glow like that. She was washing the dishes and flying around the apartment, and as she flew she glowed, and as she washed she said that she and Boris had discussed a variety of topics, including the topic of her dissertation and that the topic had changed after her first advisor died, and now the topic of her dissertation was "The Topic of Nature in the Philosophical Love Verse of the First Half of the Nineteenth Century," and that by the second half of the day, when Petia and her friends came home, they had not yet finished discussing this topic, and Yezdandukta asked Boris to stay a minute but they began discussing an entirely different topic, and Yezdandukta told him that she was very happy that her sister had a regular friend because her other friends were entirely irregular, "and you are gone all night long with them," she said to Petia, and Boris had said, "You have a very talented sister."

"When was I ever gone all night long?" asked Petia.

"You were gone two nights in a row," said Yezdandukta.

But Petia didn't say that she had gone to Boris's those two nights and that she had lied up till now, that earlier she had been lying, but now she was not lying, that she loves Boris and he loves her and that they had loved each other two nights in a row and that she had lied about the birthday party; and instead of the things she didn't say, she said:

"Did you feed him soup?"

"I hope you are not in love," said Yezdandukta.

"With whom?" asked Petia.

"With Boris, say."

Petia asked "Which Boris?" simply because she couldn't talk to Yezdandukta about her Boris but could easily have talked to her about Boris Godunov or about Boris and Gleb[5] or about a generic Boris. But Yezdandukta didn't want to talk about a generic Boris and started again talking about Petia's Boris, and Petia accidentally let slip, "You are probably in love with him yourself."

And suddenly Yezdandukta, all serious and quiet, answered her: "If he loved me as a person just a little bit, I would be willing to love him forever."

Petia had not anticipated this.

"What do you mean, as a person?" she asked.

"Just what I said," said Yezdandukta.

A huge moon was shining in the window—we know what kind of bird this moon is, we know nothing—Petia went to her room, jingling the medals, and a diamond sparkled in the moonlight like it was the sunlight, and love was like friendship, sister like brother, mother like father, a fool like a fool, and before going to sleep, Petia thought that when she dreams of Boris—not as a person but as an object or an animal, such as a can or a turtle—in her sleep she always knows for sure that this can or turtle is Boris, and she relates to them not as she would to a can or a turtle but as she would to a person—"Is that what Yezdandukta was talking about?" thought Petia. But that's not what Yezdandukta was talking about.

And then she started missing Boris so much that she got depressed, and not just about Boris but about one's place of residence, one's country, where nothing could be changed because if everything started being changed radically, if everything became private property except for the borders, which belong to the state, this couldn't be done peacefully and everyone would fight and kill one another, and why couldn't the borders be opened so that she and Boris could go to, say, Japan (say it to whom?) with a show of his sculptures and then come back in a year and paint a painting or maybe start painting it in Japan and at least finish it in Moscow, and why does just going to Japan have to take half your life, because first you have to graduate and then you have to get hired-admitted-recommended-whatnotted; and as for Japan, where the culture developed something awesome over the three hundred years that the borders were closed—well, Japan is small, it's an island and a disciple of China, whereas we are part of the continent, part of Asia and Europe, and our culture isn't sleeping either—it's just that life is dying out. We live like enemies and all that's left for us to do is fool around. It's a rare country, where no one lives because everyone's struggling, a country of experiments—but life is not an experiment; life is the only life for life. All around there are Little Oktiabrists in place of children, Young Communists in place of youth, members in place of people. Petia thought that Boris put the Kolomensky Temple in a box on purpose, so that it couldn't be seen from the outside and could only be seen from the inside. And while Petia was lying in bed, unable to sleep because she was exhausted from all these thoughts, Boris, who was exhausted at the airport, fell asleep, because he kept being unable to fly out with his temple in a box, and not even to Japan but to an Asia that was merely Central.

It would be wrong to say that Boris flew out of Moscow early in the morning; he simply flew away from a dead city, like its soul. He had purposely not told Petia that he had to leave because he really wanted to leave by plane and he remembered how he didn't leave by train when he told her that he had to leave. But he left Petia the key to his apartment, and Yezdandukta said that she would give it to her that night along with his regards, but whereas she gave Petia his regards, she decided to wait until morning to give her the key. And while Petia slept the morning away, Yezdandukta didn't waste a minute. She arrived at Boris's with the intention of instituting her version of beautification: to arrange the chairs beautifully and fold the linen. She got so carried away in her cleaning that after she washed the floors and the dishes she started on the windows. She got them to such a transparent state that the street started looking especially disgusting through the transparently clean quasi-basement windows. She moved the sculptures aside, and everything that had been moving around and jingling was now standing still and silent. When Yezdandukta returned home in the evening, she started methodically telling Petia about her day, but Petia was rushing her with her questions because Petia was impatient to find out where Boris was, but Yezdandukta had no patience for being interrupted by Petia when she was talking, and because Yezdandukta wanted to tell everything in order and Petia's disorderly questions interrupted her, Yezdandukta lost her train of thought in the most interesting place in the story, where she was talking about the airplane, because when Petia interrupted her with the question "How could he fly out?" and Yezdandukta answered

"The usual way—on an airplane" and Petia started asking questions—"When did he fly out?" "On what airplane?"—and finally Petia said: "There is no way he could have flown out on an airplane." At first Yezdandukta was at a loss for words, but then answered calmly, "He flew out yesterday, and he landed today."

"But why did he go by airplane?" said Petia.

This made Yezdandukta laugh. "How else was he supposed to get to Central Asia—by train?"

"Why Central Asia?" asked Petia. "He should have taken the train to Riga."

"That's correct. The train goes to Riga, and the airplane goes to Tashkent."

Petia immediately started hating the airplane that goes to Tashkent and has already landed—not because it was stuffed to the gills, and not because it had dirty seats that don't get aired out or disinfected, not even because there are cockroaches running and flies flying around in the airplane—flies in the air while the airplane is in the air—but because it was a means of transportation that takes off and lands quickly and conveniently—"Use the services of Aeroflot; it is always at your service"—she hated it for these services, and even though there is service on the train too, there is more humanity in a train, and if you ask, like a human being, "don't leave," it won't leave, while the plane will leave like an ass, and there is even more humanity in automobiles because if you ask a taxi, "Don't leave," it definitely won't leave, but the most inhumane means of transportation is your very own pair of feet, which can carry you away like wings.

After the airplane, Yezdandukta didn't even remember about the keys, and Petia didn't ask, and Yezdandukta didn't say, and Petia never knew. She remembered about the keys after Petia had left, and she decided that she'd tell Petia when she came home, especially since she'd told Petia before she left, "Don't be late coming home." At school Petia went to a seminar, which was devoted to the work of a male writer who was Kostroma's classmate and a female poet who was Petia's classmate, and the seminar was led by a young male critic, an upperclassman who said right away that when the heroine of a story is referred to by her last name and the hero by his first name, that's bad, and it's better when the heroine is referred to by her first name and the hero by his last name, and it's better still when the heroine is referred to not by her full name but by her nickname, like Tania in-

33

stead of Tatiana. This proved to be the most germane topic because no one said anything on any other topic. And only at the very end did someone say that the young poet's work had a manly strength to it, and then in parting someone called the female poet an accomplished poet. Following this depressing experience, Petia and Kostroma walked out into the yard, where the one who was awakened by the Decembrists and then awakened someone else himself was standing.[6]

"Shouldn't have gone around waking each other up," said Kostroma, pointing at the statue, which was small and ugly, with three tulips growing out of its muddy shoes and a hose stuck between its legs.

Then they discussed the topics of who awakened whom and who slept more and who slept less, and "Napoleon slept very little—only three hours a day—but walked around a lot, always out in the battlefield," and "There was someone else who would only sleep during the day and then keep everyone else awake at night," and "Nowadays people like to sleep a lot, and if they didn't have to go to work, no one would ever stir," and "Why would they stir—there's no point to it—you might as well sleep."

Dyl came up. "What are you sitting here for?" he said. "Let's go." And they went. How clean was the air, how good it smelled.

"What's this smell?"

"Thyme."

"Like you've smelled thyme?"

"Like you bet."

"Like where?"

"Like at the drugstore," and there was such longing for everything to be precisely clean and good, and not precise, like at the drugstore. Petia got rid of Dyl and Kostroma quickly so she could go look in Boris's windows, which were transparent like glass and dirty like the air. Boris had flown away, and everything was meaningless, and there was no place to go, and Petia went home.

It was already late at night when Yezdandukta said, "I completely forgot—Boris left you his keys."

"When?" asked Petia.

"There you go again," said Yezdandukta, "asking pointless questions."

"What questions?" said Petia because she was very nervous.

"Stupid ones," answered Yezdandukta and went to bed.

Petia didn't go to bed for a long time, but spent a long time sitting in the kitchen and wanting to ask her sister about the details, but Yezdandukta stayed away. But as soon as she came out of her room, Petia asked her, "When did he leave the keys for me?"

"Yesterday," said Yezdandukta. "Oh, and I didn't tell you—" and then she said something so frightening that Petia shivered: "I went to his house today and cleaned up a little—but that probably doesn't make any difference to you."

"That's different," said Petia. "So how was it?"

"Fine," said Yezdandukta and went back into her room.

"Everything will be all right," thought Petia as she was falling asleep. "Everything will be wonderful." And the wonder took her away all right, to a wonderful place far, far away, not so far from home, into the area of sleep, which area could expect precipitation and light frosts in some spots, and all the handicapped spots were occupied, and where there was spot color in the most interesting spot in the dream, where Boris usually appeared, he had not yet appeared, and for the first time in their relationship, he was to appear not at the point where space intersected with time, not at the point where two o'clock in the afternoon intersected with Gogol Boulevard, not at the point where the clock said five-oh-five near the zoo, but he was to appear at the time of the rain— on time—and he could have been on the street, out at sea, or in a café, anywhere where she would have found him at the time of her dream, say, at three o'clock. But he was nowhere in the dream, not at four o'clock, not at five, and only when it was nine o'clock instead of seven, and the door was closing behind Yezdandukta, did all this early-morning activity, which was crowding into Petia's head along with the sunlight and the alarm, cause Boris to appear.

At first, Petia didn't believe that it was really him; he could have been in the air or in Central Asia, but his standing in the doorway seemed so improbable that it seemed more probable that this was a dream in which she dreamt that she woke up and the fact that the furnishings in this dream were the same as in waking life meant nothing. And only when Boris started talking to her sister and Petia sat up in bed did it become clear that this was indeed Boris talking and Petia was indeed sitting up in bed. This was no dream. She threw on a robe and went out into the kitchen.

She wanted to kiss Boris, but not in front of her sister. The three of them had coffee together, but they didn't have a real conversation on any issue, because Petia and Boris had their own issues, and Yezdandukta and Boris had theirs, and Petia and Yezdandukta had theirs, which was that they didn't discuss any issue because they didn't discuss the issue of relatives (of which they had none), and they didn't discuss the issue of love (of which they had none), and they almost never discussed any literary issues, and various issues of homemaking were unpleasant issues, although sometimes they had discussions like: "Did you buy it?"—"I didn't buy it."—"Why not?"—"They didn't have any."

Yezdandukta left for work, but Petia was so afraid that she might come back at any moment that she said to Boris, "Maybe we should go to your house?"

"Were you there while I was gone?"

"Didn't get around to it."

But Petia said that her sister had gotten around to it and had even gotten around to cleaning up a little. Boris wasn't happy to hear this and was even less happy to hear that Yezdandukta had heard nothing about Petia's love.

"Why are you keeping me in hiding?" asked Boris.

"She wouldn't believe me anyway."

For a minute Boris forgot about his problems because Petia started kissing him, and then he forgot everything because Petia remembered to tell him her dream.

"Just imagine," she said. "We didn't have to decide on a place, we didn't have to agree exactly about whether we're meeting on the boulevard or at the Metro station; we only had to set a time, say, for example, "Let's meet at three," and wherever you are at three, that's where I'd be. Imagine if that were true."

He said, "Great," because it was great that they had connected, and the point of their connection wasn't a boulevard or a movie theater but the most tender point, which was so inflamed that there could be no comparison at this point, and from Boris's point of view, all of Petia was in this point, which became the point of departure for the rest of her body, which extended in all directions from this point, as though pushed by a centrifugal force, and from Petia's point of view, her whole body was directed toward that point, as though pushed by another, centripetal, force, and when she no longer had the strength to contain this force, she said "That's it," because she had come to this point and he had led her to this point. Time rolled over and out, and he said "I'm going to go" when Petia asked, "Where are you going? And what about me?"

"You sleep some more." And indeed, he left, and indeed, she fell asleep, and in her sleep she heard a ring, which in reality was a telephone ring, and it was her sister ringing.

"Did Boris leave?" asked Yezdandukta.

"A long time ago," answered Petia.

"I made some soup, I'll take it over to him."

Petia didn't try to determine where exactly Yezdandukta had made the soup—on the Metro or at work—but she marveled at the idea of homemakers who make soup right at the station.

"Don't worry about it," said Petia. "I made some soup myself. I'll just let it cool a little and take it over to him."

"You made soup?" Yezdandukta's voice expressed genuine surprise.

And so as to not make her sister angry, Petia said amicably, "So you just keep working and don't worry—I'll take it over to him myself."

"I'll be home soon," said Yezdandukta and hung up.

And Petia started cooking soup with amazing speed. And cabbage and carrots started cooking at this speed along with potatoes, which were cooking at the same speed with which Petia was circling the pot, poking carrots with a knife—Is it cooked or isn't it?—and she still had the onions, which had to be sautéed separately, together with the tomatoes—which she didn't have. Finally, the carrots became tender and the onions golden, and it all became soup, which didn't have time to cool before Yezdandukta, who was going to "be home soon," came home. So Petia placed the little pot into a bigger pot into a cold tub, but all this was cooling so slowly that she took the small narrow pot and placed it into a wider pot and placed the shower head on the bottom of the wide pot and turned on the cold water, and when the soup had cooled off in the shower and a carrot started spinning in a one-liter glass jar, it looked like an aquarium with exotic fish that had to be fed, and Petia sprinkled some parsley on top, and when she was already on her way out the door, she bumped into her sister on her way in the door, and said, "There's soup I made in the pot."

And Boris wasn't at all surprised to get Petia's soup, and maybe he wasn't happy either. But they were both happy when, finding themselves at the end of the line to get into the Yakor restaurant, they were told that they would get served but that they should warn people not to get in line behind them. An hour later they were allowed to come in and were warned that there wouldn't be time to serve them before the clean-up hour but that during the clean-up hour they would be given appetizers and wine and that after the clean-up hour they would be given the hot dish. And there was something else to be happy about: Those who'd had time to eat before the clean-up hour all left, the restaurant emptied out and began to resemble a deserted beach as well as the pages of French writers—Maupassant, Proust—as well as Russian writers—Bunin, and everyone else. And this was something to be happy about until a woman with a broom and a dustpan showed up and started sweeping under the tables, and Petia said to Boris, "What do you want to bet that she'll say 'Lift your feet up'"?

But she didn't. Bent at the waist, she moved through the room without a sound. She was the wife of an alcoholic, the mother of two, the grandmother of three, the aunt of one, and the bearer of a noble old name—which was a coincidence. And the fact that there wasn't even a hint of fish[7] in this restaurant, and the fact that there wasn't even a hint of winter outside, and the fact that the cleaning woman was worn and dirty and the waitress was all skinny and weak and was poking the champagne bottle open so awkwardly, and the fact that there were sturgeon bones hidden under the slice of sturgeon for an unknown reason—the reasons for all of this were unknown to anyone except the *sovietikuses,*[8] who knew the reasons for this whole setup. The wine was called European, and it was a cheap, faceless wine, which may as well have been called Asian, African, American—"When did they discover Australia"—"In the 19th cent."—or it could have been called 19th Cent. Australian wine—this wine was wine as a concept, just wine, not wine as a generalization that encompasses a variety of wines, the same way the cognac was a concept, just cognac, and there was only one vodka. And not just in the restaurant—right next door, in life, what was fruit? it was apples on the store shelves. The stores, unlike flora and fauna, were completely devoid of distinctions of species, order or breed, and there was only one salami, which had no variations, species, orders or breeds. But there were so many names of dishes on the menu! And if one imagined that each dish had a taste and a substance, then the appetizers were tasty and the dinner was substantial. Petia poked at the caviar and licked it off the egg, without really tasting its substance. On the menu of Soviet life, as on this menu, names served as substitutes for substance; for example, a sweet name like "Sturgeon Baked in a Pot" was, in substance, pieces of some tasteless mystery fish that could only resemble sturgeon in someone's very active imagination. But wine and champagne can inflame the imagination to such a degree that everything seems very tasty, and even sober cold stew seems drunk and aromatic. It's not like they'd come here to eat after all! then why? just to hang out. They could have eaten at home—half a liter of soup each. But they hung out until people started coming; after the cleanup hour, there were as many people there as if they'd been showing a Western.

Petia and Boris left the restaurant to the sounds of an orchestra that was playing something that might well have been the anthem of the Soviet Union. The backdrop against which they were human beings was a street, and it was inconsequential that it was Gorky Street, because what was Gorky today had been Tverskaya yesterday and would be La-la tomorrow, and everything would end and everything would change, and the only thing that would remain would be beauty (the landmark examples of art and architecture)—no, only love would remain, as the poet said when he was speaking the truth, and since the time when he said this—a hundred years later—love has remained, while revolution has come and gone, leaving behind flags, prisons, and monuments, and the cult[9] came and went, leaving behind monuments that were like prisons (and not at all like landmark examples of art and architecture), and what will be left tomorrow? flags?

3

On the last night before the New Year, having begged a book off of Kostroma just for the night, Petia had conscientiously digested it by morning, and only in the morning did it become clear to her that at the very beginning of the book Martin had received an anglophile upbringing so that in the end he would become a hero by moving to Russia despite the fact that the memories of it he had brought with him were of automobiles, tennis, soccer, rubber balls, and baths, which he liked, rather than the Pushkin nanny with her knitting and Russian folk wisdom, sayings and riddles, which he didn't like. The book was a faint copy that had fallen victim to a binding job that hid parts of the words, forcing the reader to guess that -ch was which and -nt was runt, if only because cunt would be as distant from the writer's mind as he was from Russia.[10] But the book's appearance—the absence of margins, the ratty binding, the faint print—were so appropriate to its content, its pitifulness amplifying the nostalgia for Russia that, maybe, the publisher could have made some money by releasing some bad copies. And in the morning, when Petia's eyes began closing of their own accord, she thought that it wouldn't be so easy to make books badly at Ardis,[11] where they were used to making books well, but this "bad" book was so "alive" that Petia thought with tenderness of all that was bad but "alive": the ceiling, which was overly "alive" with its cracks and water stains, the wallpaper, the plumbing, and all sorts of little things, and she was already falling asleep when the telephone cut in with a ring that was so alive that it could only mean two things: that her sister wasn't home, since she wasn't picking up, and that it was her sister calling, since she knew that Petia would pick up, which Petia did.

"Did you finish it?"

"Oh, it's you," said Petia.

"Let's say one o'clock at the school," said Kostroma.

Petia tried to postpone the meeting until five, but because this was not an ordinary day but New Year's eve, Kostroma said, "No, five would be too late. The book's not mine."

"All right, then three," said Petia.

So they settled on three. But before three Petia couldn't fall asleep because the thought of having to be there at three wouldn't let her sleep, and she called Kostroma a couple of times to reschedule for one, but Kostroma wasn't there and she got angry at the complete futility of such a meeting on such an important day. In addition to this meeting, she had two important things to do: pick up the holiday food bonus at Yezdandukta's office, sew metal decorations on her dress, and meet Boris, with whom she had planned to bring in the New Year with Yezdandukta.

The meeting took place at three o'clock: Petia handed over the book, Kostroma put it in his bag, and this would have been the end of it if Kostroma hadn't asked, "Where are you headed now?"

"I have to pick up the food bonus at my sister's."

"And then what?"

"Finish the dress." So Petia told him about the dress: that it was made of pieces of fur and silk and was supposed to have these metal decorations that she hadn't had time to sew on. "What about you?" she asked.

"I'm going to Dyl's. We could go together."

"Where is he?"

"In the city center."

Petia called from a pay phone and everything fell into place: Yezdandukta had already gotten the bonus, and Boris would come at eleven.

"Let's go," she said, because there was still time.

But it turned out that Dyl resided not in the city center but in the center of the outskirts, because after they got there they kept going and going until they got to a huge Stalin-era building that was the only such building in the area. There was a park across from it, and in the park there was a monument. They entered the building, but not from the main entrance side but from the side where there was a stairway attached, and at first they had to go up this stairway to a door, which Kostroma opened to a stairway that went sharply down, into total darkness, where there was a door. Kostroma knocked and Dyl opened the door. This could hardly have been described as a room. But there were curtains and there were beds— for some reason, there were four of them, and in the middle there was a old-fashioned painted school desk, and on the walls over the beds there were those things that they put flags into, and when Kostroma came in, he said, "Why did you stick sticks in the flaginas?" because there were fir tree branches sticking out of the holes.

"Because," answered Dyl.

"You gonna sleep on needles?"

"I'll sleep on another one."

Petia walked around and looked around and this was not a room but something gross, and she just asked Dyl, "Why are there so many beds?"

"So four people can live here," Dyl explained.

"Who do you live with?" asked Petia, who had never before been interested in Dyl's life.

"By myself," answered Dyl. "But I pay for four."

"So you pay four times as much?"

"No, twice as much."

41

"Why?" Petia was surprised. "If it's five rubles for one, then it should be twenty for four."

"I pay thirty."

"So you pay more than four times as much?"

"No. Exactly twice as much, because it's fifteen each."

"I wonder who rents this out."

Kostroma got some fabulous bottle out of his bag, and at this point Petia may have lost interest because she didn't repeat the question and Dyl didn't repeat the answer.

Kostroma started opening the beautiful vessel while Petia opened the curtains to discover that there were no windows and the curtains covered bare walls.

"There are no windows," said Dyl.

"That's scary," said Petia.

"I was scared too. That's why I put up the curtains."

Dyl, who was so pretty, living in such an unpretty place was not a pretty picture.

"Where did you live before?"

"On the shore," joked Dyl, but, jokes aside, he could have lived on the shore before.

It was hard to be joyous in such a joyless place, and Kostroma, who may have been trying to get Petia to enjoy herself, said that he and Dyl had decided to make an andy-baby. She started asking about the andy-baby, and Kostroma started explaining that he and Dyl wanted a baby but they weren't homos and Dyl wasn't a woman and Kostroma wasn't a girl and by March they would track down a black chicken and steal its egg, and whoever got to it first would fertilize this egg or maybe they'd both shoot into it, and then they'd look after this egg and then they'd have a monster of their own, and then they'd be happy, whereas now they were unhappy without an andy-baby. And when Kostroma wrote *android* in Greek, Petia realized that she was getting limp from the port and then she managed to think *borisus* in Latin, whereupon she fell asleep. As it happened, there were one too many beds and in his sleep Dyl thought that he saw Kostroma sleeping on two beds at the same time in two bodies, but of the three of them Kostroma was the only one who didn't sleep at all that night, on any bed and in any body. At first he thought that he should wake up Petia and take her home and then he thought that it would be better not to think about it.

Anything can be the case except what cannot be the case. At

midnight the clock's hands kept going but Petrarka didn't come. So Boris and Yezdandukta filled their glasses. And had a drink. And wished each other—what? A Happy New Year, that's what. That's the kind of holiday it is—people drink, wish each other a Happy New Year, and go home. Which they didn't. Supper ensued. The two of them ate everything, and went to bed with full stomachs. He screwed Petrarka's sister, and there can be no memory of this. Boris remembered this around six in the morning, in a three-ruble private car, around eight. He and Yezdandukta had woken up in the same bed and he hadn't even known what to say to her, the same way that he hadn't known what to say to her before he did it, and he did it because he didn't know what else to say, but after he did it, he didn't know what else to do or what to say, so he fell asleep and by the time he woke up there was nothing left to do and nothing left to say. And when the car stopped at a light and he looked up at the red light, he remembered it all in this light: that Yezdandukta had been a virgin. He even remembered her admission that he was her first. She dropped it so matter-of-factly that it sounded like people get new hymens every year and at that moment it sounded to him like he was her first of the new year, which was understandable, especially since the clock hand had only gone halfway around. But now he suddenly realized that this admission was not made in the new year, that it was made in general. There had been every sign that he was her first. The only sign that had been missing was he himself. He had clearly been absent from this incident and from what she said and he said and she asked and he said and, after saying it, fell asleep. A virgin at thirty-five in the new year at forty in '85, and in the mouth too.

Still, it's odd that everything can be going on one way, going along and then stopping and then something else entirely starts going on. Petia opened her eyes but it was so dark and there was no sign of light so she shut her eyes. Then she opened them again, and again it was dark. In this darkness, where she couldn't see anything, she understood where she was. And stirred. Then a light went on, but it was small. And the people were small and their shadows were big. And the shadows were smoking. These enlarged shadows exhaled and the smoke was a shadow of itself.

"We slept through the New Year," said Kostroma.

"What time is it?" asked Petia.

"Seven o'clock of the first."

"The first what?"

"The first of '85."

"Idiot," said Petia.

She said it and started crying. She cried so hard that it was hard for Kostroma and hard even for Dyl. She cried at the desk, smearing her makeup all over her face, she slumped over the desk with her face in her sleeve and shoved Kostroma with her elbow when he tried to sit down next to her, and then, after crying her eyes out, she slammed the desk top.

"Is there water here?" she asked Dyl.

"Over there," he said.

And she went over there. Over there was a toilet and a shower—all stuffed into one closet, all trashed and fucked-up but she didn't give a fuck.

"Take me home," Petia asked Kostroma.

"You just fell asleep," said Kostroma. "What's so terrible about that? You'll tell him, he'll understand."

She said "Idiot" again and he quit trying to comfort her. But he took her home, where Yezdandukta opened the door and Kostroma left. Yezdandukta had no intention of concealing anything. She told everything right away, but everything seemed so unbelievable that Petia didn't believe her. Yezdandukta said that she'd never done anything with anyone and that Boris was her first and that they did it that night for the first time. Petia was shocked that Yezdandukta and Boris had done it, but the very assertion that her sister was a virgin was shocking. This was more an aspersion than an assertion. And Petia sat down in the kitchen and stayed sitting. And then later she was in her room and stayed lying. And she tried to think but she couldn't think of anything. She thought that she wouldn't have killed her even if Yezdandukta weren't her sister, because Yezdandukta was an idea and how could you kill an idea? And another idea: He didn't want to but she wanted to and it all just happened, she didn't want to and he wanted to, and it happened, they both didn't want to and it happened. She tortured herself like that.

After spending half the day in bed like this, having cried her eyes out, washed up, and then started crying again by evening, Petia was saying to herself, "But I love him, I love him terribly, and he loves me, and we love each other, so why is everything so awful?" She went to Boris's, and it was not even clear how she got there: when she left the house, she didn't know that she was going to Boris's, and when she answered her sister's question by saying "For a walk," she had no idea that she was going to his house. It took her a rather long time of using different means of transportation, which didn't even represent the fastest way of getting there, and at first she was not even going to his house but in his general direction. And once she found herself in his general vicinity, she then somehow found herself at his house, and when she saw that his light was on, she got so happy that when she showed up on his doorstep she was boundlessly happy. Boris was surprised at all this happiness, which he didn't understand. There is only one way to say "I love you" but there are many different ways to say "I'm angry," because there aren't many reasons to say "I love you"—in fact, there is only one reason, which is love— whereas there are many reasons to say "I'm angry"—too many to say them all at once. Boris at once said he wanted to know the reason Petia hadn't come on New Year's, and Petia immediately said the reason was that she "just fell asleep." This reason didn't sound like the main reason to him and it sounded to him like the main reason was behind this reason, and the main reason was that she was "really sleepy." None of this was any reason not to come to New Year's, but there was no other reason. But when Petia told Boris that she knew everything because her sister had told her everything and begged Boris to give her just one reason this happened, Boris said, "I don't even know—no reason."

That this was followed by "love" was bad—that is, during "love" it was "good," but it didn't get better after love. And even after Petia swore to Boris that she loved him and only him and would never love another, this promise didn't make Boris feel better, because it would have been better without this promise because he had felt better earlier, when she didn't say this and things were good. And when she asked, "Is this good for you?" and he said, "It's good," this wasn't the best answer, and when after this she said, "But do you feel better now?" and he said, "Maybe better," she thought that really he felt worse because she herself felt worse, and she decided to go home, because she thought that would be better.

And when she was going home alone because she'd said there was no need to take her home and no need to catch a cab, and when she got off the Metro, she was horrified by the thought of how horribly she wanted to stop loving him. She knew that she loved him and only him and would never love another. That's exactly why she wanted to stop loving him—so that she would never love anyone else. She knew for a fact that she would never love another, and so she wanted to stop loving him forever. She decided that she would try her hardest to stop loving him so that she would never love anyone else. And this powerful thought sapped all her energy, and she fell asleep because she didn't have the energy to read more than a few pages by a powerful writer from a powerless country.

4

What began as a joke for Dyl and Kostroma soon became no laughing matter, namely the matter of acquiring an andy-baby. It is a fact that the first day of a March moon occurs in March. There has never been a March that didn't have a March moon. And there has never been a moon that didn't exist in March. Kostroma bought the chicken ahead of time at a bird market, albeit a black market, since the chicken also had to be black. He took it to his grandfather's dacha and kept it in his room. But it wasn't laying anything. At least it hadn't laid any yet. Kostroma reported this to Dyl, who became concerned: "Think it's dyed?"

"Why would it be dyed?"

"Think it's old?"

"What difference would it make whether it's young or old? I was thinking, maybe it's a hermaphrodite?"

"I doubt it," said Dyl. "Let's wait a bit more—maybe it will lay one. If not, we'll sell it and get another one."

So they waited. Nothing. The next Sunday Dyl went to the market, but even the black market didn't have any black chickens. They decided not to sell the chicken but to wait for the first day of the March moon. As the calendar would have it, this day coincided with the grandfather's birthday. Kostroma was surprised at the coincidence. But Dyl said that this was no coincidence because if they'd decided to make the andy-baby the previous year then the days wouldn't have coincided, because the first day of the March moon moves around while grandfather's birthday stays in place, and the following year they wouldn't coincide either.

"But we decided to make the andy-baby this year," said Kostroma. "So it's a coincidence."

It started snowing. They were standing in the garden in front of the dacha, looking up at the sky in which they couldn't see the moon, which was hanging around somewhere behind the clouds.

"There isn't any coincidence because nothing's going to happen," said Dyl. "Have we got an egg?"

"It will get laid—today."

"What's the occasion for that—your grandfather's birthday? I'd completely cancel birthdays for grandfathers like that."

"And what would the occasion for that be?"

"The occasion of his putting my grandmother and grandfather you know where."

"As a member of the Party, he was carrying out the orders of the party."

"I'd cancel birthdays for parties like that too."

Suddenly there was a flicker of the moon in the sky under the snow—that is, it looked like it was snowing right on the moon. And then they heard so much clucking that Dyl and Kostroma ran from the garden and into the house. And sure enough—there was an egg. It was full like the moon and it even had some smoky clouds which looked like moon mountains that you can look at from Earth. And Dyl chickened out.

"Well, maybe, the hell with it," he said.

"Why don't you do it in honor of your grandmother and grandfather?" Kostroma teased him. "Not only are you not reliable enough to become a member of the Party, you are not reliable enough for anything else, either. Sit down and jerk off while I suck the egg white out of the egg."

"Why do I have to be the one who jerks off?"

"What are we going to do—jerk off together? I can't come looking at you."

"I can't come at all."

"Then we shouldn't have gotten into this andy-baby business at all. It said clearly: *Fill with male sperm.*"

"Why don't you do it?" Dyl pleaded. "I can't."

Kostroma got under the blanket and started doing what had to be done. And while he was doing it, he thought of Petia, but he didn't want to implicate her in this dirty business, so he started thinking of her separately from the business, and as he thought of her, the business advanced, but as soon as he thought of the andy-baby, his spirits flagged. So then, to be finished with this business, he thought about this one whore who had told him in the middle of doing it that she had things to do, so he finished his business while thinking about the whore's business. Kostroma showed his sperm to Dyl, but Dyl was so preoccupied with sucking the egg white out of the egg that he responded with a perfectly businesslike "Good job."

It turned out that it's easy to start loving and not at all easy to stop loving: Petia had fallen in love with Boris for no reason and she had to stop loving him for a reason and this wasn't so easy. When Petia loved Boris, she didn't realize how many things she loved about him; she didn't love his appearance and his actions and his talent separately because she loved him wholly, as in *borisus*. But when she decided she should stop loving him, she had to stop loving everything separately—his face separately from his art, separately from everything else. When she told herself that she didn't love his face and didn't love kissing his face, she started loving his art even more and was ready to start kissing the Kolomensky Temple in a box. But when she told herself that she no longer loved his art, that it had all been done before in art, that she loved the art of the canon, then she wanted more than anything else to love him separately from his art and against all canons. Basically, Petia didn't know how to stop loving Boris. Sometimes it seemed to her that this was simply impossible, and then she started hating him because she loved him so much. Love had been but one feeling, but trying to stop loving him turned into a bottomless pit of feelings. Basically, trying to stop loving felt the worst, worse than any feeling, except, maybe, the feeling of having no feelings.

She got worse. The first time she got worse was when she found herself at Dyl's for the second time. His hole in the wall hadn't changed a bit, except what was now sticking out of the flaginas looked less like branches and more like sticks, and the desk had been shoved over to the side, but the curtains were the same and everything else was the same and in the same place. On their way there Dyl had told Petia that soon he and Kostroma would have their own andy-baby—"Remember, Kostroma told you at New Year's?" Reminding Petia about New Year's was a crime on Dyl's part, but for her part, Petia shouldn't have been going all the way out to Dyl's place, because Dyl's place was the scene of the crime, because it had been a crime on her part not to come home for New Year's.

"Tell me about it," said Petia.

And Dyl happily started telling her that the andy-baby was growing and would soon be hatched, and then they'd be happy.

The egg was sitting in a pile of manure, and they'd eaten the chicken.

"Did you kill it?"

"It happened all wrong," said Dyl. "Kostroma and I had planned to kill her the right way, like you're supposed to."

"Which is how?"

"Which is how it says in the book, the manual for slaughtering domestic animals, but his grandfather got there ahead of us. It tells you everything: The right way to kill a cow, a chicken, a pig, so it's not painful for them and it's not painful for people to watch."

"So his grandfather killed it?"

"Seems like he killed her in such a brutal manner that she swallowed her tongue. I think he tortured her to get her to tell him everything."

"What?" said Petia.

"Everything she knew. You know what her skin looked like when his grandfather finished plucking her? Kostroma said it was like a mulatto's, and grandfather said he was going to make soup."

"Did you eat it?"

"I ate a little."

"Did it taste good?"

"Na-ah."

By the end of the story it was already the beginning of April, during which Petia and Boris never saw each other—that is, there was never a time in April when they ever saw each other—and so April came and went, and then came May, and as soon as Petia got to Boris's, she immediately noticed a new work of art, but she didn't ask about it immediately because she immediately asked, "Do you love me?"

"I love you," he said.

"I love you forever," said Petia. "I love you more than you love me."

"I thought you didn't love me anymore."

"I love you more than anyone else in the whole world."

"You are lying to me."

"If I stop loving you I'll never love another."

And Boris said, "You will."

And she said, "I won't."
And he said, "Yes."
And she said, "No."
And he said, "What are we arguing about?"
"I was unfaithful to you," said Petia.
"Why?"
"I did it on purpose."
"Why."
"So I'd be worse." Petia said that when everyone around her got worse she had to get worse too, and if everything got better all by itself then she'd get better too.

"It will never get better all by itself," said Boris.

"But you were unfaithful to me, too," said Petia.

"But I didn't do it on purpose," said Boris.

And during the act she demanded to know whether he'd enjoyed himself during the act with Yezdandukta—"Did you do the same thing with her as with me?"—and to shut her up, to keep her from saying another word, he put it in her mouth, and with her mouth full, she said, "I love you."

This was the last thing he heard, because when he saw that she was no longer in the room, he heard the door shut.

The fact that Boris was Petia's love and the fact that Petia was his love were indisputable. She loved him, yes. He loved her, yes. But love didn't love Petia and Boris—historically, love had not loved them. *Historically* not in the sense of stories—romantic, sentimental or realistic ones—but historically in the sense of the history to which they bore witness, and as witnesses they could testify that this historical moment was not too auspicious for their love. Of course, theoretically it's possible to love during practically any historical period, which is what they did—they loved—but love didn't love them, being historically in opposition to them, because on New Year's Eve Petia had been reading a book that could have been a household book, meaning that it would be in every household, in which case there would be no need to digest it in one night, but this book wasn't in every household or in every other household but in the other man's household, even though the writer, whom Petia loved, loved his country, which was far away from him, and the country loved its writer, who was far away from it, because both the country and the writer were Russian, but the writer distanced himself from the country, the Russian way, and the country distanced itself from the writer the

English way. And the fact that love, historically, did not love Petia and Boris, was bad; it was also bad that love loved them pornographically—meaning what?—meaning generic characters in a generic setting in the act of making love.

Suddenly, at dusk, an internal force caused the egg to explode with the andy-baby's appearance; the shell turned to dust in a single moment. There was the force, there was the shell, the shell splattered—and bang!—Kostroma had never seen anything like this, and Dyl never saw anything like it, and when Kostroma started describing it, Dyl started asking questions.

"Like dust," said Kostroma.

"You said before, like a fountain."

"It splattered like a fountain, but what was in the air was glass dust, and when the dust settled..."

"Too bad I wasn't there."

"You know car windows shatter at high speed?"

"The speed of light?"

"Not necessarily the speed of light—the speed of 80 kilometers an hour."

"Oh, yeah! Incredible speed," laughed Dyl.

"Don't you laugh. For our cars, it's incredible, and on impact, glass shatters and turns to dust."

"Regular glass?"

"No, not regular glass. I forget what it's called."

"But the shell wasn't glass. Glass is chemical, and the shell was organic."

"How do you know what the shell was made of?"

"I know."

"So what's it made of?"

"Egg shell."

"That's the thing. Seems that the andy-baby was writhing around inside the egg at incredible speed."

"You know what it's like?" asked Dyl. "Think about it." And after thinking about it, he said, "It's not like anything."

"Looks like it," concurred Kostroma.

"It's not even possible to imagine," said Dyl.

"Imagine: the shell turns to dust, and the andy-baby is standing there."

"And then what?"

"You won't let me finish," said Kostroma. "Then he disappeared somewhere. He just hatched and disappeared, and I

51

didn't even get a good look at him."

"Well, is he vertical? Like a person?"

"So what if he's vertical? A chicken is vertical too, and it stands on two feet—but it's not a person."

"But what's he look like at least?"

"I'm telling you, I didn't get a good look," said Kostroma. "I didn't have time, plus it was dusk, and what can you see in the dusk?"

What happens at dusk is testimony to the fact that nature has no color, only the concept of sunlight, the physical mystery of the eye, the shifting of the spectrum in the fog, when yellow looks reddish and green looks yellowish, and what of the traffic sign that warns of a road narrowing—does it denote the narrowing of the road in perspective rather than the physical narrowing of the road? And an object at dusk is undefined, in that it lacks clear definition—that is, its outline pulsates and the object breathes *optically* at dusk, and it is this *optical breathing*, rather than color or shape, that indicates the presence of the object and the near-absence of distinction between an inanimate object and an animate object, or the absence of—having lost its color, the chair loses its weight and its legs become thinner and the table's corners soften. And Kostroma stared at the ceiling at dusk, which arrived an hour later this time, because this time it was May and the last time it was April. He heard a radio somewhere far away, but he couldn't where it was or what it was saying. And he stretched toward the sound, and the sound turned out to be nearby, even though it sounded like the radio was somewhere far away. The sound was right next to the couch, but Kostroma was looking for the sound on the ceiling, when in fact it was on the floor, and when Kostroma shifted his eyes from the ceiling to the floor, he saw the andy-baby, who was making the very sounds that sounded like the radio. The resemblance was striking: it sounded like a distant station that's being jammed and it was impossible to tell what language it was, but it was clearly human speech, or at least speech resembling human speech. Kostroma listened to the andy-baby talking and looked at him. He was hard to hear and even harder to see, but Kostroma was able to see that he seemed to be folded in half along the nose line: in profile, the little monster looked enough like a person, but when he looked him straight in the face, he appeared as a fuzzy line, and the very concept of looking "straight in the face" became a bit fuzzy; this line had no

eyes, mouth, ears or anything. So just as Kostroma was silent be-
fore the andy-baby appeared in the room, he didn't say a word to
him, and the next day he didn't even breathe a word to Dyl, be-
cause he wanted Dyl to see and hear everything for himself, so he
said, "Let's go to my place."

"Can't hear you," said Dyl.

And Kostroma didn't say anything to that.

5

The summer was short like a winter day, like a flash in the pan,
fly-by-night; by all accounts it was soon nothing but a memory of
summer, a summer that came and went, ending as soon as it
began, like a summer shower, which was soon replaced by an au-
tumn shower, which starts during the day and lasts long enough
to cover the autumn evening, which is long enough that the rain
is frozen by morning and stays in the air like snow—no, not like
snow: it really is snow, rather than a likeness of snow, because it
is now really winter, not to be likened to anything but last winter,
which was not as cold, white, clean and good as this winter; no,
like it or not, this winter is worse than the last.

Petia still loved Boris, but she hadn't seen him since the last
time he had seen her. She didn't see Boris, but she heard a lot
about him from Yezdandukta, and Boris heard a lot about Petia
from Yezdandukta, but it's better to see once than to hear a hun-
dred times, so in late winter, when Petia heard about him from
her sister again in early spring, she went to see him that very day.

If consciousness is superficial, then what's it like? smoking is
bad for you but dying is good, good to pump the last drops of en-
ergy out of the earth, good to split the atom, good to go faster
and faster, farther and farther, to build the kind of plaster night-
mares that the future of humankind, which will be approaching
extinction, will have as a monument for the rest of its time, a
monument to power, as in nuclear power, a monument built by
whom?—well, by whom?—by us. What do we need water for? To
drink it. No, for the monument to drink it, and we can drink
what's left over, except that nothing's left over—not for us, not
for the fish, not for the flowers—but look at him, the man of the
future: naked, wearing headphones, holding a bomb because he
has armed himself in order to disarm his opponent—but who is

his opponent? he himself, disarming himself—and where is he going? he is going back from the future, into the present, and soon we are going to meet. Hello!

"Hello," said Petia to Boris.

She had accomplished a lot in a year of trying to kill her love; what was left was passion. She had pumped out the love and pumped up the passion, like in the country where we live, which is divided into fifteen colonies, which are definitely colonies, because only colonies can be pumped mercilessly like this, like from the Baikal and Siberia, from the Baltics and Ukraine—we pump everything we've annexed. And we are getting pumped like one giant colony, which consists of fifteen colonies, including oil, animals, water, hell—everything! "I can't live like this! Now what?"

"What did you say?"

"What?"

Is it nature that's sick all over? No, it's man that's sick all over himself, all over his heart—but who's healthy? Life is evaluated when it is over. We are disintegrating! Not only do we not love—we don't listen, we don't look, we don't want to see. "I can't live like this!"

"Did you say something?"

"What?"

Boris had done a new painting and had hung it up; it was simple, like all masterpieces, but it wasn't a masterpiece just because it was simple. It was painted on a magnetic piece of metal. On a light blue background that was almost white, there was a path that wound as though through the air, and in its most invulnerable spot, almost at the horizon line, Boris had attached a little island made out of thumbtacks, which flashed fiercely in the rays of the setting sun, and there were little human footprints on this path, but there was no human in the painting, as though he had just walked on the path and left fresh footprints, and it was as though he had walked on the thumbtacks as well and there were footprints on the horizon line in the corner of the painting, where the thumbtacks ended, and these footprints were all sticky, wet and bloody, and some of the thumbtacks he had stepped on were bloody too. Petia didn't tell Boris anything about her love, because her love had been a flash in the pan, fly-by-night, by all accounts it was now nothing but a memory of love, a love that came and went, ending as soon as it began, and in this memory they were both cleaner and better.

Petia walked around and looked around and said, "You've done a lot of work and gotten a lot done."

"Yeah, I've done a little work," said Boris.

"Is it true that you want to marry Yezdandukta?" asked Petia.

"Did she tell you that?" asked Boris.

"I want you to tell me."

"She is a good person," said Boris.

"Do you love her?"

"I love her as a human being."

"Remember I told you that I'll never love anyone again?" said Petia.

And Boris answered, "You will anyway."

"No," said Petia. "Never. Because I don't want to."

"Someday you'll want to anyway."

"We're going to die anyway," said Petia.

"Someday we'll die."

In the light of a sunset that was real and not painted, they were both alive and not painted, and the love that had historically not loved them was real and not pretend, and Petia and Boris hugged in a way that was simple and not complicated. They simply hugged to say good-bye, which followed hello, which had come and gone, ending as soon as it began, and after Petia left and walked a few steps on the boulevard, she returned with such passion and she and Boris started kissing until it got dark and then until it got light. And at dawn, when she was barely alive from love, Petia said to Boris, who was nearly dead, "Why am I thinking about war—why? Do you think there's going to be a war?"

"No. I try not to think."

The street sweeper started shoveling snow over their heads, as though they were underground, which in fact they were, as though he were burying them, and Petia never said to Boris "I love you" even once all night, and he didn't say "And I you."

Are we not dead because we are still alive or are we still alive because we are not yet dead?

There were many familiar faces but it was hard to tell who was who—like in a dream. And the temple, where Kostroma was standing and where people were crowding, was flooded with this cool light, and some of the grates had ice on them, and it was sad, and there were many fresh flowers, like at a funeral, and when they carried in the stretcher and were carrying it over people's heads, everyone saw a person sitting on it, and the person's face

55

was distorted by makeup—that is, part of his face was covered by a mask that had sloppily been put together of pieces of cardboard, cotton and thumbtacks, and his skin was covered with chalk. His head was out of proportion to his body, as though his body belonged to a different head or the head to a different body. And when they carried this in on the stretcher, there was a whisper—"Linen, Linen"—but the head looked nothing like the Linen on the coins or on the medals or on the posters—or the Linen on the medals looked nothing like this Linen. And then they turned off the light, and when they then directed a stream of light so that the head cast a gigantic shadow on the wall, and the shadow was the exact Linen profile, everyone recognized Linen. And they carried the stretcher around the room along the walls, and people started throwing flowers up in the air, showering Linen's shadow with the shadows of flowers. A funeral dirge sounded, and it had a vulgar twist. This twist—this vulgar effect— was created by the shattering of symbols—that is, when the cymbals came in over the tooting of the horn, the cymbals shattered into a hundred pieces. The sound of symbols shattering during a funeral dirge woke Kostroma up, and when someone pinched him hard on the thigh because he was wearing his underwear to a funeral, the pinch woke him, and he was indeed wearing underwear.

It was snowing outside the window and it was morning, while just a minute earlier in the dream it had been night. Kostroma thought about Petia and about the fact that she had many men and that different people had told him they had seen her in different cities with different men at the same time. And Kostroma thought about how different Petia was, and then he thought that she was always the same and only the men were different, and then that the men were the same and she was different. Then he thought that the cities were different, and then that the cities were the same, and then he thought the same stuff that he'd thought in the first place, except all at once—at the same time. And he was so thirsty and so loath to get up that he took a deep breath of air, which was fresh and cold, like water, and he thought that when we don't have enough water we need it like air, and when we don't have enough air, we need it like water, and when we don't have enough bread, we need it like water and air, and we can do without everything else, but he couldn't do without water so he went to take a drink and then he kept going and going and going, and then spring came and the snow began to melt and the sun began to shine and the birds began to fly and the wind began to blow and the girls began to—and Yezdandukta told Petia that she was marrying Boris in the summer.

6

Summer was at the height of summertime. No one had gone anywhere this summer: not to the seashore, not anywhere. People were walking around in the rain, carrying umbrellas to protect themselves from the rain and not from the sun, and when it started clearing, every object took on sharp definition in the sunlight, and when Yezdandukta showed up in the doorway in the morning and said "Today," Petia knew it meant that today there had been a transfer of power. And even though Boris still had power over Petia, there had been a transfer of state power, with one power structure departing and another arriving—and what was one to expect? after all, any new power structure is an unrealized old one. And the old power structure was the dark side of a love that had accomplished nothing. Let there be new life! let it be better, cleaner, and richer! let it be! long live the king after the king is dead! what does that mean? that means that Yezdandukta went from a sister to a wife, and Boris went from a lover to a husband, and Petia went from a lover to a sister—what a change!—and blood flow accelerated, the blood was rushing and flapping like a bird, and could it be that soon we would all fly? it would be better if we all took a flying leap instead of taking flight.

"Today?" Petia asked Yezdandukta. "Yesterday you told me that it would be tomorrow, and now it's today already."

This was the beginning of the end!

Petia didn't have to spend much time looking for Kostroma and Dyl; they were in place, and Petia, after informing them that it was "today," undertook a taxi offensive. The world can be conquered only by taxi—not by plane or by tank, which are the wrong means of transportation for conquering the world.

"Drivers of Taxi Park Five, do you recognize me?"

57

"Yes, yes, yes!" The world can be conquered only by the meter—a kopeck for a kopeck, a ruble for a ruble, an eye for an eye, a tooth for a tooth!

They flew in the taxi and conquered Europe, Italy, and the America that's beyond the horizon in the newspaper, the newspaper being precisely the horizon shielding everything that's beyond the horizon.

Be happy, ye conquered nations whose lives will be paid for by the meter, be healthy!

"Don't drive yourself crazy," said Kostroma to Petia. "What do you need him for—Boris!"

"I need him because, and he me, and the two of us, and if only we—"

"Don't cry," said Kostroma.

"How can it be," said Petia, "that even the smallest mistake is the end and even the smallest infidelity is the end?"

"You'll marry someone else," said Kostroma.

"Never," said Petia. "I'll never love again."

"You will so," said Kostroma.

The taxi was flying like a bird, like a plane—where are you taking me? do tell!

And when they ran out of fuel and when the driver said how much, none of the conquered people could see their conquerors, who'd made a ring around Moscow on the Ring Road; the people were carrying heavy bags to the store and full bags from the store; their arms felt like they were about to break; they walked in the rays of the setting sun, and there were red rays on their faces along with yellow and pink rays and the entire spectrum of rays to which their skin was receptive, and they walked the way that was almost the same way they had walked yesterday, thinking not about the transfer of power but about the beginning—the beginning of next week—because power had been transferred in a peaceful manner, by the meter, paid for by the passenger. Long live peace!

And the new life got under way in the way of the long-forgotten old life—like the time when Petia stayed at Boris's house for the first time and there was a whole world of stars outside the window, she stayed at his house now, but not like that time, because this time was after her sister's wedding, and the stars shone like that time, but this time Petia lay under the blanket like the sister of her married sister and Boris lay with Yezdandukta like the husband of Petia's sister. But all the sisters and brothers up in the sky, pagan ancestors' brides and grooms, were all in their own constellations, living lives that didn't change. The meaning of this is that the stars above stay the same while the people underneath change. And so they lived—Petia at Boris's instead of Boris, and Boris at Yezdandukta's instead of Petia. "What if Yezdandukta loves him like she loves me," thought Petia, "and Boris loves her like I love her, and Boris loves me like he loves me, and I love him like I love him?" Less than a month later, Petia found out what Boris's love for her was like. When Petia saw Boris in the doorway as she was already getting ready for bed, he said he had come to get the colored chalks, and he started going through the drawers but couldn't find the box. And Petia put on a sweater and started looking for the chalks too. They didn't find anything. There weren't any chalks. Petia sat down on the bed and started drinking milk out of the carton.

"Want some wine?" asked Boris.

He opened a bottle and she drank some from the bottle.

"Should I bring a glass?" asked Boris.

"Bring one for yourself."

So Petia drank out of the bottle and Boris drank out of a glass. She had no doubt that love would follow the wine. They still loved each other, despite the fact that love didn't love them—that is, they loved each other physically, not platonically—never like Plato, never like a man loves a man, never like Socrates loved Socrates—and when they had physically tired of love, Boris left and returned no less than a month later, when, physically, fall had already passed and winter had ended, when nothing could change physically in their love any longer, when at dawn one day Petia suddenly woke to the monotonous sound of a radio that was on somewhere outside the window. And she opened her eyes and saw the andy-baby—who she knew existed only because Kostroma had told her—standing in front of her. He was standing there, and she could hear that he was talking but couldn't tell what he was saying. Suddenly, he said in perfect Russian, "Hand over the medals."

"What?" said Petia.

And he repeated harshly, "Hand over the medals."

"What medals?" asked Petia, even though she got it right away: the ones that flashed in the moonlight, the ones she and Boris each had half of.

"Medals?" said Petia.

The andy-baby shot the word medals into her ear, possibly shattering her eardrum, because there was definitely an explosion in her ear. And Petia got out a sweater that was all covered with medals, and the andy-baby shook the sweater, and the medals flashed and fell to the floor with the first rays of the sun that flashed on the medals. The andy-baby got the rest of the medals without even bothering to wake up Boris; he just showed up by his bed in Petia's room, where Boris now slept, and, after toying with Boris for a bit using some easy-listening music, he branded Boris's memory with seven exact-time beeps, which made Boris shiver in his sleep, but it was as if the andy-baby had never been there.

Coming upon a sleeping Kostroma, the andy-baby got closer and got talkative.

"Go knock off your grandfather."

"No," said Kostroma.

"He is a bastard," said the andy-baby.

"I'm not the bastard to knock off a bastard."

"He knocked people off," said the andy-baby. "Go knock him off."

"Then it will never end: we started this knocking people off and we can stop, because it's time to knock off knocking people off."

"Then I'll knock you off."

"Knock it off."

And the andy-baby pierced Kostroma's body with the pins from the medals. He used the medals to pin his insides to his skin. And he used the diamond pin to pierce his heart. And he dragged him down to the river and let him go with the current. And Kostroma started floating. He floated in the gasoline circles, which were plentiful in the water. And when Kostroma's funeral was over, when his body had floated off and the cries of the people seeing his body off had almost faded, because it was already late winter, his body, floating into the distance, was covered with junk—with Little Oktiabrist star pins and Young Communist pins and factory pins all over, all over other unprecious metals, all over at the end of March.

PART TWO

1

Only after you get a license should you learn to drive, and only after you marry should you fall in love, and only after you have built communism should you feed the people, only to do this you should graduate from high school and only then get into college.

When Petia was in love with Boris, she wanted terribly to fall out of love with him so that she would not love anyone, and when she fell in love with Gleb O.R., she wanted terribly not to fall out of love with him so that then she would not fall in love with someone else. Gleb O.R., Boris? Gleb or Boris? Everything bad about Gleb O.R. was human, so you could say he wasn't a bad man. And everything good about Petia was feminine, so you could say that she was a good woman. And this is wonderful, it is wonderful when the weather is wonderful and the sky is full of the last remaining, the most exotic sparrows, because all the other sparrows have become extinct while airplanes and satellites keep reproducing; they are strong and made of steel, they feel good in the sky, they impress the eye with their birdlike flight, and life is wonderful and all our republics make us proud and they don't even have the right to self-determination, they cannot secede to the right or the left, they can only go straight up in the air; when they are shot down in the air like a mirage, like imaginary territory with imaginary borders, all the republics, after seceding straight up, will cry gassy tears from tear gas—you say that people suffer on Earth, they suffer themselves and they make all other forms of life suffer, and if every person taken separately is right, then for some reason all people taken together are not right, but life is good in Luxembourg, and what about the Soviet Union—is that good too?—it is good too because we are all patriots while they are all just people, you say, "It's a good salad, but it's got something that doesn't belong in it,"—"what doesn't belong in it is that something is missing," and there is no milk today, it comes with tomorrow's date on it while the newspaper is dated yesterday, what is it about our lives that doesn't belong, what is missing? what doesn't belong is that something is missing, and there is no sun today, and the weather comes with tomorrow's date on it while life is dated yesterday.

Now this is really something, two holidays in one: The Day of Workers Solidarity and the day of Christ's resurrection.[12] "Christ has risen!" "Indeed he has," but we've got May First and Second off. Dear communist atheist worker, Christ has risen! Honorable Christian, you fasted and ate no meat all through spring, and now happy May Day to you, happy Workers Solidarity Day.

"Christ has risen!"

"Happy May Day!"

When Petia fell out of love with Boris, his image faded in her memory and even his features faded so much that she did not even try to recover them, because now her image of him bore a vague resemblance to a real person, to Boris, whom she once loved. And so that she would not totally forget that she really had loved him once, that is, so as not to forget the very fact of love, she forgot him totally, in his entirety, so that all that was left of her feeling was dead knowledge. He remained in her memory like a fossil and the love itself fossilized in her memory, there was nothing lifelike in this love, and when Petia told Gleb O.R. about this, he thought about it and said, "This is what always happens when people don't love each other anymore."

"You mean our love could become fossilized if we stop loving each other?"

"Any love can become fossilized."

"That's exactly why I don't want to stop loving you, and I shouldn't have wanted to stop loving Boris so much, because what difference does it make whether it's Boris or Gleb O.R."

Gleb O.R. laughed. In general he often laughed when others would not have thought something funny, but he in particular thought it was, and in general, traits that in other people generally seem negative seemed positive in Gleb O.R. in particular. And Petia did not take offense, and she just asked,

"You don't want to stop loving me for the same reason?"

"For a completely different reason," said Gleb O.R.

And Petia did not know what this reason was, and it might be that Gleb O.R. himself did not know either and it might be that he laughed for no reason the same way that he loved for no reason.

There was harmony in their love: Petia did not love Gleb O.R. precisely as much as he did not love her. Whenever she started loving him less and her feelings seemed about to run out, she sensed that Gleb O.R. too was loving her a little less, not like before. If he had continued to love her as much as before, a love of such magnitude could have become a burden to her, but this did not happen: as soon as her feelings for him weakened, his feelings for her became weaker too, but then when she fell in love with him again, he immediately fell in love with her with an equal force. Whenever Petia left Gleb O.R., this did not mean that she went back to another man. She did not have a choice between Gleb O.R. and someone else. She had only Gleb or Gleb O.R. And whenever they came together, they felt a sharp desire for each other and a dull ache after being apart, but then they had a sharp pain after being apart and a dull desire to come together again. "You are a monster," Gleb O.R. would sometimes say to her. "I can't be that much of a monster," Petia would comfort herself, "if he still loves me."

And for this love to continue, for it to be permanent, they could not be together continuously, so they would separate. They separated in order to come together again. And they came together in order to separate again. But their comings together brought them so much joy and their partings brought them so much sadness that their love was alternately sad and joyous. They had been together for a year, but they had also been separating for a year, so if you added up all the hours they had spent together in the course of the year, you would end up with only three days of continuous togetherness. And this brings us to our main point: that one (fine?) day they decided to go away forever for three days so that during three consecutive days they could spend together all the time they had spent together in a year. And these three days...

Gleb O.R. brought a map of the Soviet Union and pointed at random; he chose a place out of thin air, though airspace was not on the map. Gleb O.R. was big and hairy, and to a certain extent he resembled an ape, to the extent that an ape resembles a human being at all.

"I'm not going there," said Petia. "By the time we get there it may secede, and we'll end up abroad."

"Theoretically, any republic could secede."

While they argued, they covered themselves with a newspaper so they wouldn't freeze, being naked, and as they rustled, as they loved each other, page one of *Pravda* became outdated because it was a different year now, and a different day. The weather was inclement, so they flew to their republic by train, which flies even in inclement weather. It was nice on the train: there was no ticket checker, and the passport checker let them into a two-person compartment without checking their passports for a marriage stamp. They ended up in the compartment together, as both lovers and passengers, as Monsieur and Madame. They weren't allowed to do anything in the compartment—no drinking, no smoking; they closed the door and opened the window. Trees and houses were rushing backwards on wheels, and all of life was concentrated along the railroad tracks. Behind the foreground of houses there was only the background of fields and forests. The hotel on wheels was rocking in its sleep. Only after they had not had enough sleep did they arrive. The sky was gray and low, and this low gray sky only hinted at a tall blue one behind it, as though one color showed through another, blue through gray; a wind was blowing. And while Petia and Gleb O.R. got lost here, while the Earth was rushing along with the force of so many horsepower, where a unit of measurement is a horsepower so as to create a vivid image of the Earth rushing in a horse-driven carriage and galloping around the Sun, which also gallops in a carriage around that which attracts it. And the power of the car engine was also measured in horsepower, and it was carrying them down a road that was attracted to a house, but leading right up to the house was a different road, a narrow and overgrown one, on which it was impossible to go at high speed, and Petia and Gleb O.R. walked on foot past dusty eucalyptus trees and giant chickens. The owner of the house herself had many children, and those children had many children. And next to the big house they were shown to a small house, where everything was small, even though there was plenty of room. The windows looked out on this and that and the here and there, and in addition to the windows there was also a door, and it was a mere formality that you opened the door to enter and you opened the windows to look. The window was for contemplating, for being in a certain spot but letting your eye travel far, and the door was for following your eye yourself. So they entered the house. In the morning they were awakened by the clear sound of music, which was coming down off the mountains as though there were a grand piano on the top of the mountain, and the whiteness of the keys and the snow, the black lacquer of the piano and its great blue shadow filled the soul with the sweet sounds that were scattered in the air, that birds were carrying, that were coming down the mountain along with the cool air. But the people who were coming toward the house were not carrying these sounds; they were bringing noise.

"What's out there?"

"They are like birds," Gleb O.R. said. "They wake up and start babbling."

But the people were not just screaming like birds gathered in a flock; what was written on their banners was not innocent bird babble, and they had flown in not just to do some screaming and go home, and theirs was not some sort of bird bazaar but a politically pointed bazaar. All together they shouted "Down with!" and "Hail to!" And even a birdbrain could have understood "down with!" what and "hail to!" what—down with the old, hail to the new, good morning!

And then it grew brighter and hotter, and the sun in the crowd grew hotter, and the crowd grew stronger in its heat, and in its zenith were the leaders, separating from the crowd and becoming more and more noticeable, their voices rang louder and louder, and when there was a knock at the door, Gleb O.R. could hardly believe his voice when it asked meekly:

"Who's there?"

"Open up!"

"It's open," said Gleb O.R.

And the sun and the heat in its zenith entered the room along with five people, as it were. And as they entered, as they looked at one another, as they sat down, as they started to speak, the stream of their words was like a mountain stream, which is unstoppable, and Petia and Gleb O.R. swam with the current in this force of nature of words. And when they ended up foreigners at the end of the speech, Gleb O.R. said, "That's all!" to stem the flow of their speech. "The republic has seceded, the land has been looted, the rivers are poisoned, when we eat cucumbers we calculate the amount of poison we've eaten, but cucumbers are not the point: in personal life a divorce is a disaster, and so should a divorce be a disaster when you are quibbling over borders rather than a two-room apartment. And if we want to start living a simple patriarchal life with sheep and grape arbors, without a first-rate ballet or the first man in space, that is, so that the future is like the past."

"And we are going to go home," said Petia. "It's that simple."

But everything turned out not to be so simple; everything turned out clever and complicated. These five clever emissaries started being cleverly cunning, but Gleb O.R. was not taken in by their cunning, and he thought that by being simple he was being

67

the most cunning.

Their conversation reached a dead end; they started talking about poetry.

"But you are a poet?"

"Who?" said Gleb O.R. "I do not take part in politics, that is, like any citizen, I live the life of my country, but my life is the poetic form, the structure of verse, not the political regime or the form of power... Don't you think that the poetic form is the closest to perfection: civilizations collapse, and so do regimes; but we know a strict poetic form—say, the sonnet—and the free form—blank verse—and both are perfect forms, we know strict political regimes—dictatorships—and we know free regimes—democracies—but neither of them is perfect."

"Of course, and this constitutes your consent to our proposal," the most cunning of the emissaries said sweetly. "We declare a republic that will be perfect in form and content, like a poem, which can be perfect in form and in content, and the laws must be so significant in their content that they will be perfect in form."

"But that is absurd! Absurdity in poetry is not so bad, but absurdity in life is worse."

Gleb O.R. had such a memorable appearance that, having remembered him once, you wouldn't forget him. He could not, for example, have been a spy, and he was not one.

If one had to describe his appearance in two words, then those two words would be *magnified Chinese*, and that would convey the most accurate image of his appearance. It was as if a Chinese man had been enlarged proportionately to make Gleb O.R. And when strangers, lots of them, met Gleb O.R., many of them had the fantasy that they had met him somewhere before. But when they looked at him more closely, they saw a Chinese man, an ordinary man but increased in size. Gleb O.R. had a height that would perhaps be natural for an American or a Swede but was a bit large for a Chinese man, and to go with his height he had little eyes, acceptable for the Japanese, the Chinese and some other ethnic groups, but a bit small for a European. The same was true of his nose: it was a bit flat; whereas his hands were, despite his large feet, small. He was steadfast and resilient like a Chinese man, but he often proved maladjusted like a European, and he was often steadfast in his maladjustment.

"Some getaway," said Petia.

"Yes, we can't get away," said Gleb O.R.

"This is stupid," he said when the emissaries had left, leaving Gleb O.R. to sleep on it. He had to think and say yes. And when Gleb O.R. poked his head outside the door, he discovered an honor guard, which told him respectfully that it would be better not to poke out before morning.

Still, Gleb O.R. poked his head outside one more time after Petia fell asleep, after the love he had cajoled her into, though it was a burden to her after all the burdensome conversation. The young guy from the honor guard accepted the cigarette offered by Gleb O.R. Sitting down on the stoop, they smoked and started talking.

"I'm not going to go anywhere," said Gleb O.R., "but it's stupid to hold me here. I can't even make one woman happy, never mind an entire nation."

"It is nearly impossible to make a woman happy," said the guard. "So there is no point wasting energy. It's easier to make an entire nation happy. When a man and a woman are equal, it's no good, and when a man gives a woman freedom, it's terrible if she takes advantage of it. But there is nothing better than freedom and equality."

"Why don't you just add brotherhood to the list, so I could love her like a brother, like a fag," said Gleb O.R., clearly angry.

But the good-natured young guard paid no attention and went on with his good-natured speech: "Plus, no leader has ever been happy in his personal life, and power over an entire nation is a way to reduce stress—it's impossible to have power over this one single person, and the leader satisfies his desires by having power over an entire nation, not being able to satisfy his desires with one person, it's easier to satisfy everyone than someone."

The guard had been assigned to Gleb O.R. especially so that Gleb O.R. and his views would ripen overnight like fruit and would fall into the hands of the people with the first rays of the sun, filled with the juice of love for it. Gleb O.R. returned to the room as unripe as he had gone out green.

Petia was lying in bed like a spy: she had not only heard it all, but she had heard it all from Gleb O.R. before—that he couldn't make her happy.

What else was spy-like about Petia, was: narrow dark glasses to keep the light from the desk lamp out of her eyes, a pair of shorts with lots of pockets, which she had stuffed with a variety of neces-

69

sary items, namely: a pen knife, a flask, and an address book with so many telephone numbers that if one were to dial all of them consecutively the ringing in one's ears would not cease for a week. When he saw her outfitted like that, Gleb O.R. asked no questions because he knew that this was the way it should be. They jumped out the window, passed the guard, who was real but asleep and whose watch said one-oh-three in his sleep, and ended up on the other side of the fence, where a horse stood harnessed to three cars; after giving the horse some food they got on it, hijacking the three cars in tow. The last two, which broke off and crashed, well, they crashed, but the one that remained at the end of the horse—Petia straddled this one, letting the horse go; she got behind the wheel and started to race, and Gleb O.R. sat beside her and swung from side to side like he was in a kibitka, even though Petia was as careful with him as one would be with the heir to the throne. Gleb O.R. did not tolerate cars well, and he did not much like the fact the Petia loved cars. But for all of his remarks she had a single remark: there is nothing better than speed and fast driving. She said in the last century she would in any case have been a horsewoman like Turgenev's young heroines, but that in any case in the twentieth century Turgenev's young heroines as well as Countess Mary and Anna Karenina would be driving cars.[13] Gleb O.R. was arguing no longer; he was nauseated from such fast driving, and he thought of horses, which don't smell like gasoline, and of "giddy-up!" in place of the gas pedal, and of "whoa!" in place of the brake, and all that appealed to him a lot more. But the whole thing together—Petia as a spy driving him—appealed to him no less. She drove the car to a dead end, a place so dark and wild that it was wild and dark.

When they say "In the name of the country!" without regard for the wishes of a small republic, then the country is in the wrong; when they say "In the name of the republic!" without regard for the wishes of a family, then the republic is in the wrong; when they say "In the name of the family!" without regard for the wishes of the person, then the family is in the wrong and the person is in the right because the smallest element turns out to be the largest and the largest the smallest. But the worst part is not that a word can have several meanings but that a meaning can be used to mean several things. What is the meaning of good? it is in the variety of meanings, in the sense that when opposite meanings that different people see in the meaning of good exclude

70

each other, the meaning of good loses all meaning, unless it ac-
quires a figurative meaning. The night was at night level, and at
moon level there was the moon, and then there were the sub-
levels of stars, each of which was at its own level—an indescribable
view of the world—and a person with eyes. Waves rolled up to the
feet, and feet rolled the waves away, and all things separate were
together. Together with all, separate from itself. And one wanted
to think tenderly of everything dear to the heart. And a heart that
aches for all the world is not like a liver that aches because it is
filled with bile, because a heartache is many blows to the heart. It
beats stronger than the sea, that is, stronger than the waves, with
a frequency approaching the frequency of waves when the wind
blows—but more frequent than that. It is ready to jump out, like a
wave out of the sea, and it is inside the chest. And everything
dear to the heart is like the first time, and there is no feeling that
has ever been felt before.

And when the car door slammed, when Petia felt the gust of
wind, when Gleb O.R. started coming down to the sea after her, a
bird sitting in the water in the moonlight tore itself off the
branch along with its shadow, and when it flew upward, tearing it-
self away from the shadow along with the branch, it was no
longer clear where all this came from—their leaving and going
and coming and leaving and coming—no, not even that, that is,
not where did that come from, but this, all of this at this mo-
ment—where did it come from? From the same place as life (eter-
nal life?) after death and first love come from. Because, though
the second love is chronologically second, it is still first-rate, and
one could use the case of the second love to describe, in this case,
life after death, of which we have no memory, as we have no
memory of the first love, from beginning to end, from the first
kiss to the last, and this isn't because there was no first love but
because there was too much of it, and therefore it is forgotten
completely. Here we are alive today, but which life is it? There is
no such thing as time, of course. Because night and day are not
time but the presence and absence of the sun, and we do not re-
member our first love in the same way that we will forget our sec-
ond as long as it is not our last. When Petia fell in love for the sec-
ond time, everything that was happening with Gleb O.R. seemed
to be happening for the first time. And when she had never
kissed until she kissed Gleb O.R., when she kissed him for the
first time, when she had never been held by anyone, because be-

71

fore we were born for the first time, how many times had we died? And when Petia and Gleb O.R. went back to the car so they would not freeze in the love of the moon, he started doing to her what she loved most with him, and before him, which was not so convenient to do in the car but he saw that she loved it terribly right then, as always, and those three words they kept repeating, and when she turned her face to him he seemed to think she looked vulgar in the moonlight and her eyes glistened horribly when she said, "That's it." And the sight of a certain part of her clothing that had gotten stuck on the steering wheel seemed, somehow, a little strange.

"Where are you going?" Petia asked.

"Just a minute," said Gleb O.R., and it started to rain.

The rain was lashing at the roof and the windows and when Gleb O.R. returned and handed Petia her shoes, which somehow ended up in the front seat, while Petia herself was in the back seat, and he said the word love to her for the first time, though maybe he said it to her for the hundredth time, but for the hundredth time he said it to her for the first time.

And when I fall in love again for the third time, always and never, will it be the same thing one more time? she took another swig from the flask, and thoughts came rushing from the drink, which was running out.

"I don't want to stop loving you so that I never love anyone again," said Petia.

And Gleb O.R. said, "Go to sleep."

And there was an onrushing tide of stars, their stasis in the splayed-out sky, which is in no way influenced by the Earth, not by its status in the luminary community, not by its attraction to the Sun, not by anything at all. And every woman subconsciously identifies either with the Virgin Mary or with Mary Magdalene, one of the one, one of the two, and if one of them was the mother of Christ and the lover of God, then the second was the one who loved Christ so much that after him she could not love any other man. But is it possible to love any other man after Christ? Is it possible to be unfaithful to Christ with some other man? And if it is possible, then with what kind of man would it be? one who is alive? and if it is possible, then why? because he is alive? and if Christ has risen, then where is he now? And they did it this way on purpose, so that two women who are so different should have the same name—Mary—so that the choice is between

72

white and white, between black and black, between good and good, between evil and evil, between Mary and Mary. And both of them, the two of them, *knew Him.*

This cool, this cool coming down from the mountains, was filled with the vice of happiness, which was not serene. As long as Petia slept on Gleb O.R.'s arm, she could not conceive the child of God, but anyone who was without sin could throw stones at her. In her sleep she was more like Magdalene, filled in her sleep with a passion for the opposite sex, which in her sleep was not personified—she did not see Gleb O.R. in her sleep—she was an abstract woman with a passion for an abstract man, and she slept until the torrent of stones thrown at the car holding the whore in its belly broke the glass. Gleb O.R. jumped out of the car. He was thrown back. He stood like a monument with his arms bent backward, because esthetically the monument has no need of them because it has no place to put them. Some beast shook the car from behind, and while the car stood there completely disgraced, with its trunk open and four of them rummaging in it with their behinds sticking out, Gleb O.R. said, "beasts."

"Where?" screamed one, half stuck in the trunk.

"What?" asked Gleb O.R., not knowing what? and where? He got hit on the mouth and when he heard "here!", he was thrown back with such force that before the force of friction could do its business he was rolling with the force of swinging and the force of slipping. The car lurched forward, turned around and lurched forward—back to the city, and Gleb O.R. lurched backward toward the sheet of paper that had fallen out of the trunk and that called for peace, love and liberty and in which simple ideas were accompanied by such vague ideas that there was no point in trying to work through them. And the fog came in. Gleb O.R. sat in the fog with the sheet of paper, which contained the following design—tire tracks over the appeal: "We stand for liberty, but the term liberty to us means not the dependence but the independence from a small group of liberated people who force upon us the kind of liberty that is not liberty but dependence on them." Gleb O.R. was wondering. While he was wondering about one thing, everything started happening at once. Along with the coming fog came people—out of the fog. And Gleb O.R. was in such a fog that they took him by the hand and led him. Then, though he was alive, they showered him with flowers as though he had been a dead man, and when he was dead on his feet with exhaustion they brought him into town with music and ceremony. He was installed in the same old garden, the same old house, the same old room. As soon as he lay down, a young man entered the room and sat down, and his appearance was so remarkable that it deserves to be described in detail. He sat down and Gleb O.R. sat up so he could get a better look at him.

"Cricket," someone in the garden called for the young man. He put his ear to the door and listened.

"Cricket," someone gave a bit of a scream through the window, and then at the bottom of the garden someone gave a bit of a whistle.

Cricket opened the curtain a bit and when his eyes got used to the dark a bit, he recognized someone from his group, but after thinking a bit he realized that he had not been recognized in the dark after all, so he lowered his head a bit and sat down on the chair for a bit, and Gleb O.R. lay down again for a bit.

Cricket was only third-generation Russian, and in all other generations he was Ethiopian because the Russian tsar had brought his great-grandfather to Russia as a present.[14] As what kind of present? a little Negro, a little person, a little parrot? and what if Ethiopians are all that talented and if they are imported into Russia they could become the source of national pride and only Ethiopians will be able to write the encyclopedia of Russian life?

Cricket had little interest in politics, but even though he had taken no part in any of the bloody demonstrations, he was exiled from the capital to Middle Russia. And the picture he encountered there was an indescribably beautiful picture. This natural landscape contained everything that can possibly awe a person. And there was not a single person anywhere in sight, except for the one who was taking in the beautiful sights. And the human eye itself, cast into the distance, inspired awe in the beholder of this eye.

The house stood on a bit of a hill, and in front of the house a field opened itself up, and behind the field a stream glistened, and behind the stream there was a grove, and as soon as it occurred to Cricket that the picture lacked sound, a train passed by in the distance, past the stream, and the clatter of the train was sweeter than music. The picture was truly wonderful, and on the hill to the right one could see the golden dome of a church, and as soon as it started to get dark and the dome faded, the moon came up over the river. As an Ethiopian, Cricket was astonished by this picture, but he expressed his immediate astonishment as a Russian, giving his entire soul over to poetry... His Russian was simple and pure because the Russian language, which became his native language, was given to him as a gift, the exact same way that his great-grandfather was a gift to the Russian tsar. And gifts, however simple, are beyond doubt, while work, however diligent, is not. But Cricket was also distinguished by his mind and his diligence; and he achieved such power over the Russian language he received as a gift that when verbs overpowered him, he was able to put them in their place and tense. The same with the names of things—because his mind immediately seized upon the primal nature of these things, he had no fear of placing tears alongside fears, which the experienced Russian mind, weary of the familiar sameness of native sounds, would have feared... And when Cricket wrote, "The devil tricked me into being born in Russia"[15] —this would have been funny coming from a Russian because where else is he going to be born if not in Russia, but it was not funny coming from an Ethiopian. He saw what he heard and what he heard, he saw. He wanted to travel abroad, but not in the way that Russians travel, to air out their eyes and ears, but to take a rest from his motherland, as one takes a rest from one's family. But the border, it turned out, was closed to him, so he decided to marry and bury himself in family life.

On the eve of the wedding he organized a bachelor party, to avoid being too sad or too happy. Of course he married for love and was happy with his wife like a simple person, but as a complex person he could not find happiness in the family. And when Gleb O.R. got a better look at Cricket, he noted that he was no longer a young man but a tired married man—as well as a major poet. And this marvelous corner of the earth, where the only problem was that the weather had gotten bad—the southern sun was replaced by a northern sun and consequently southern rain was replaced by a northern rain and the southern sea by a northern sea—lay waiting for a historical figure who was entirely recognizable and known precisely by virtue of his unremarkable nature; he was neither intelligent nor stupid, of German heritage but better that he be English and better still that he be American, and best of all that he be a most ordinary Frenchman. And as soon as they say where he was born, everyone will know who he is, and when they say how he died everyone will know who he was, and as soon as they say what he did everyone will know that only he could have done it. Napoleon brought fame to St. Helena, Pushkin brought fame to D'Anthès, and the Decembrists brought fame to December.[16]

But this must be a historical figure who did not bring fame to a particular period or place or person but who became famous himself thanks to a certain period or place or person, and this was how he became a part of history. But considering that we have historic place and historic time aplenty, we clearly lack historical characters, so let us turn to fictional ones. Petia and Gleb O.R. went away not in order to separate but in order to be together all the time, and when this time was taken away from them, it stopped all passage of time, including historical and geological time. And if there was a war on, it froze until they came together, and if there was a genius who was developing, his development would stop until they came together. Time stopped at precisely the hour when Petia was separated from Gleb O.R. And Gleb O.R. did not even think that something could happen to Petia while she was not around because how can something happen while wheels grind to a halt, wars freeze and geniuses stop developing. And when Petia hitch-hiked into town, when she flagged down passing cars because they were passing with the passage of time, which had stopped, when she did this because the car in which she had been taken away as a spy stalled at the very first stop line, Gleb O.R. showed her Cricket, who had fallen asleep somewhere in the middle of his historic time. And as soon as Petia and Gleb O.R. came together, wars started up again, as did the rain, which seemed to have stopped. Events began to unfold with the force that propelled those events.

After Cricket left, moving slowly but inexorably toward his duel, and they were left alone together in the room, Gleb O.R. said the following:

"He will be killed. You'll see."

She looked off into the distance, and in the distance there was the sky, darkened by the rain, and in the sky fates were being decided.

"If he is Ethiopian by background, if his great-grandfather was given to the Russian tsar, if he was exiled from the capital and not allowed to travel abroad, if he married and did not find happiness, then he will be killed in a duel. But if, for example, he was born in Corsica and conquered all of Europe, then he will die on

St. Helena and his remains will be carried across the ocean," said Gleb O.R.

"And if you were born in Simbirsk and exiled abroad, were a good swimmer, married and never had children, then you will lead a revolution and die on Sparrow Hills,"[17] suggested Petia.

Gleb O.R. did not say anything to this because what Petia said was politics whereas what he had said was history. Gleb O.R. was happy discussing history but unhappy discussing politics, because if you say that you don't like Napoleon or Peter the Great, you won't have to go to prison, but if you say that you don't like Lenin, you might. Gleb O.R. did not want to go to prison, where he would have bad food and a hard bed and where he would spend his best years uselessly.

And the sky, its length and its width and its length multiplied by its width, which would make thousands of km. sq., and multiplied by its height, which would make thousands of km. cu., was without stars, it just was.

All the power was concentrated in Gleb O.R.'s hands—he belonged to the people with an awful force, just as the people belonged to him with an awful force. The people saw that he was not hungry for power, and this was most likely why power was hungry for him. And the way people can be hungry for blood, they were hungry for a speech. Gleb O.R. did not know what to say. Everything he wanted to say, he said in his poems. The people were literally coming to a boil. The people were the masses. They were not each person separately but a mass of bodies, a solid mass of life, one in its sweat; at times a distinct arm, foot or head poked out of the mass—the mass was walking on its feet and moving its arms, there were heads rolling over the mass of heads, and then they drowned in the general mass. In its density, the way the mass rolled forward and rolled backward, the people resembled a heavy liquid; this liquid was hard to push through. Petia was pushing through, pushing forward, and the mass was pushing her back. One could easily drown. Not just Petia but anyone could have drowned in the human mass. It is remarkable that water cannot drown in water because it is homogenous, but a person can drown in human mass even though it is homogenous. Gleb O.R. dully started to recite poetry. The effect was astounding: the human mass, like a heavy liquid of high density, clearly reacted (chemically?) under the influence of—temperature? oxygen? light?—the mass was clearly consuming oxygen and producing hydrogen, and plants, which were intended by nature to consume hydrogen and produce oxygen, were nowhere around, and the crowd started choking on its breath and running around the corner to breathe out. The force of poetry flagged: the forces of nature had no use for it. If Christ has risen, then where is he now? Lord, humans are not prized these days, and maybe they are not humans if they have no human rights, maybe they are a heavy human mass. People can be written off. They'll be written off by the system. Our human is the most defenseless of humans, he burns and drowns, while people in general tan and swim, his only defenders are his mama and his papa, and he is defenseless like an elephant. But if elephants are being exterminated for ivory so the Japanese can make trinkets, then why are we exterminating humans? because it doesn't make you sad? because there are lots of people and not a lot of elephants? because elephants are born every four years and humans every nine months? humans more often than elephants? something is not right! Lord, let them hang themselves on their gas pipelines if a single baby has to burn in this gas, and the Kazakhs are not cattle for radiation experiments, why did they replace the nobility with the *nomenklatura*, oh, Lord? because because why? and that if the director of a fish farm is caught stealing, he will become the director of a Young Pioneer camp, and if he is caught stealing, he will become the director of an home for the handicapped, and if he is caught stealing, he will become the director of a pet store; he is a wandering director like the Wandering Jew, except one wouldn't want to be a fish, a Young Pioneer or a handicapped person along his wandering path.

But perhaps humans deserve the life they live, perhaps they would get bored with a pastoral view of pretty cows and meadows, the way Adam and Eve got bored in the absence of sin—humans get bored without sin, and if humans did not get mangled on buses and in lines, if they were not evil, then they would not be good and would not learn to fly—not because they have no feathers, not because they are not meant to, but because—because. Petia was pushed up toward the podium, and Gleb O.R. pulled her up on it. Cricket read after Gleb O.R., and because the crowd of listeners had thinned and the mass had become more liquid and Cricket continued to read, it seemed like he was reading for the clouds and the sun—the wandering listeners. One would be hard pressed to say whether his poetry was good. It was probably very good and mainly it was impossible to evaluate: one listener might have said that this was good poetry, but this would have said more about him as a person than it did about the poetry, the same way that someone who said it was bad poetry would have said more about himself than about the poetry. Petia and Gleb O.R. got down from the podium. They settled in their room, and Petia, who did not know what to say to cheer Gleb O.R. up after such a fiasco, said, "It's just business as usual."

What was business as usual? the demonstration, the poetry, tear gas and other gases, corpses and dry rations! One could say that about anything: one could listen to the radio or watch television and see how people suffer and make all forms of life on Earth suffer— is this business as usual?

"Are you coming to the dance?" they entered the room without knocking and then there was such a knock at the door, such a knock-knock, and after two knocks two people entered. This was the official invitation to the dance.

What is a novel without a dance, and what is a heart without love of the dance—there can be no such novel and no such heart. And there can be no dance without a novel, and what is a dance with no love for the heart!

"What's with the dance," Gleb O.R. said, twisting the invitation for two in his hands after the two times two equalled the invitation and left, the four of them—what kind of dance can there suddenly be in the midst of such general insanity.

"It's just business as usual," said Petia. "In the time of the Directoire," and she recounted for Gleb O.R. a story she had heard from him, which we won't bother recounting.

Petia was preparing for the dance the way a bird prepares for migration, carefully cleaning her feathers and storing up her beauty. Gleb O.R. got a toothache. The tooth ached beneath his cheek and then it started aching in his heart and stomach as well. Gleb O.R. finally broke down and complained.

"You should see a dentist," Petia suggested.

It was a wise suggestion. Gleb O.R. ran away from his pain. It's a good thing that dentists go on working even after factories have stopped working. Gleb O.R. opened his mouth and showed himself in all his splendor. Unlike a kangaroo, Gleb O.R. would never have died of hunger because his teeth got ground down—he would have gotten new ones put in—and no human being is going to die of toothless hunger, because people die of death while kangaroos die of hunger, and nobody is going to give a kangaroo false teeth, until the kangaroo becomes a human being and gets them himself, but when is that ever going to happen? it's not so long now; when once again there aren't any televisions or anything on Earth, nothing except pyramids because pyramids are for eternity and televisions are for pleasure, because pleasure passes but eternity stays—for your pleasure. The dentist put a cotton pad on Gleb O.R.'s tooth and told him to eat nothing for two hours. It was a top-level dance. Literally—it was up in the mountains, virtually up in the clouds. And as the toothache quieted down, the music began playing. Gleb O.R. sat out the first dance, as he sat out the second and third. He did not dance. First Petia danced with Nicholas. And when Gleb O.R. saw her with Nicholas and saw the impermissible ways he was holding her, ways that were permissible in the dance, that is, when he realized that this was not merely the first Nicholas with whom Petia was dancing but Nicholas the First, he immediately understood that this was the historical figure who would shoot Cricket, because Cricket was driven to his death by the tsar, and the tsar was Nicholas the First.[18] Everything around them receded: the mountains, the trees and the precipices seemed immaterial, as though they were made of something like air and flew away like smoke. They were like the morning fog, and this was that sort of environment. Petia and Nicholas were flying. He threw her and caught her; she flew away and returned. Underwater, that is, in a substance like water, they swam to and fro. The music for their dance included the knocking sound of a receding train, and the whistle of an airplane, which whistled when Nicholas clicked his heels together. And the sound of thunder and the honking of cars and ships in the distance—all of it was music. And Petia said, "Sire," and Nicholas said, "Madam!" He was of pure Russian blood, there was not even a bit of Tatar blood, well, maybe there was some Tatar, but there was no German blood, and even if there was German blood, there was certainly no American blood mixed in. Yes, they were dancing in this environment, amid transparent H_2O, no one could derive a formula for the sort of environment this was, and at midnight on Thursday all the mountains took their places: row to row, mountaintop to mountaintop, formula to formula, and the sea rolled in, wave to wave. This took place in the above-mentioned environment, and it took place yesterday, on the summer solstice, when the day lasts exactly one day and the night lasts exactly one night, when the day does not draw its length from the shortness of the night; and after this day the long days started becoming short, and to make a long story short, there was less light and more dark. And Gleb O.R., who was not dancing, looked at Petia, who was dancing, and at Nicholas, who was dancing, and at everything that was swimming and laughing and rejoicing and sparkling, at everything that was ding-a-ling—he took another scalding drink and started dancing. And when he saw that Petia was still dancing with Nicholas, he sobered up, but as soon as he embraced her, he was drunk again. Unlike Nicholas, who was light on his feet, Gleb O.R. was heavy. He pulled down on Petia on the three-quarter beat and the six-eighths. If dancing with Nicholas was like running downhill, then dancing with Gleb O.R. was like going uphill, and the hill kept getting steeper and steeper. And then he saw that he was climbing this hill all alone, and Petia was no longer in his embrace because she was now embraced, perhaps, by the horizon. And while Gleb O.R. was pondering this, he lost sight of her entirely because she had disappeared somewhere with Nicholas, and when he found her backstage, they were talking politics. Backstage at the dance there were wars, demonstrations and a few picnics. Monarchs sat at the table divvying up imaginary borders on the map, while real people were divvying up real borders on the ground, and monarchs were losing sleep while people really lost their heads, livers and hearts, when their heads bounced off as though they were made of rubber and their other parts fell off as though made of rags. History retained the names of the monarchs and the total number of heads, while the total number of stomachs, livers, legs and eyes lost in wars was astronomically high, so only astronomers knew the number of individual organs lost in the war. Gleb O.R. used his power to issue a decree forbidding duels and forbidding Nicholas the First to dance with Petia, and forbidding the dance altogether, and because the dentist had forbidden him to eat, he decreed that the formal supper be given out as dry rations. And while the guests, who had left the dance, were chewing on their crackers and prying their cans open up in the mountains, Petia unleashed a torrent of tears onto Gleb O.R., saying that he had spoiled the dance for her. He could see that she hated him, that she couldn't stand the sight of him, and he couldn't stand the sight of that.

"You are a dictator," she said to him. "You spoiled tonight for

81

me."

But using affectionate flattery and flattering affection, he got her to admit that she did not want to fall out of love with him so that she would not fall in love with someone else.

"Who, Nicholas," Gleb O.R. asked. "The First?"

"The Second," said Petia. "What difference does it make—it could just as well be Alexander."

The decree was accompanied by a set of instructions. These instructions not only forbade Petia to dance with Nicholas but forbade her to dance at all. She read the instructions in one sitting, the way one reads a spy novel but not the way one reads poetry, savoring every line. When she finished reading she knew she was not allowed to go anywhere, that the house and the garden territory were the only places she was allowed to inhabit. Sometimes your dreams have a way of coming true very quickly. Gleb O.R. had long dreamed of putting Petia on a desert island so that she couldn't go anywhere, and now she had nowhere to go. The house they now inhabited did not even slightly resemble a palace, and the republic, which had seceded, did not seem at all foreign, and Gleb O.R. barely resembled a monarch, and everything else, come to that—the sun, the sky, the stars and the trees—resembled themselves only to the extent necessary to forget about them altogether. Petia was missing northern stars, the cold and dull sort, and these hot and bright ones hurt her eyes, and the chirping of exotic birds hurt her ears. Petia was missing sparrows.

"I'm sick of this," she said.

"You and your whims," he said.

They were drinking cognac and eating cottage cheese—perfectly disgusting: either the food was completely unsuitable or the drink didn't suit the food, but the cow had not yet come home to be milked by its owner so they could buy the milk. And the garden did not at all resemble a royal garden: in one corner somebody was listening to the radio, in another corner a woman was screaming at a dog; "maybe we should declare a hunger strike?"—it is wise to declare hunger strikes when there is nothing to eat. Maybe we should become vegetarians, since we have nothing to eat? all those vegetarians aren't as noble as they pretend to be: they don't eat meat but they eat the most defenseless of creatures, those who can't speak—if they are mute, does that mean we can eat them? fish, vegetables and fruit, and especially fish, which won't scream the way meat will. Gleb O.R. was jealous of

Nicholas the way one monarch gets jealous of another. And if Napoleon had been around, he would have been jealous of Napoleon, and if Pushkin had surfaced, he would have been jealous of him as a poet. As soon as the cotton pad dried up, Gleb O.R.'s toothache came back. He got up to go see the dentist. Petia said, "I'll come with you." At least Gleb O.R. was not jealous of the dentist: there was no rivalry between him and the dentist. The dentist sort of put Gleb O.R. to sleep as he looked in his mouth. Petia was watching the dentist's mouth and hanging on his every word, of which there were not many, and these were light and airy. He who was nothing became everything, and he who was somebody disappeared.[19] The dentist had never been anything else; he had always been a dentist and only that. He was a dentist under any regime. His heart did not waiver in choosing its allegiances. He was. He extracted and he implanted. He built bridges. He covered rivers. There are people all around, and who are these people? they are all Soviet people. There are no millionaires except for the underground ones. Everyone dreams of meat and a car. They get up in the middle of the night to make it to work by morning. They shove and are shoved when they go, and they shove and are shoved when they come back; they are shoved in the stores, they are sunned in Sochi, and they are rained on in the movie theater. They are so angry with one another, and their anger is so strong, and it can come to such a boiling point that they will say things over which they could kill one another. There are more and more criminals and fewer and fewer geniuses because criminals develop their crime but geniuses do not develop their genius, and cities develop and grow, and the names of cities develop: Leninabad, Leninsk, Leninogorsk, all headed up by Leningrad, which was constructed by Peter. The dentist was in every way a middling sort of man, not like the Middle Ages, which are memorable, and not like Middle Russia. He told Gleb O.R. to come back tomorrow and sent him on his way. At home Petia held Gleb O.R. and told him sweet nothings. They were playing king and queen, boy and girl, drunk slavemaster and young girl slave.

That which is obscene but pleasurable is as moral as a dream. She was fully dressed, and he was fully undressed. Nor was she wearing anything extraneous. A boy who desires a girl, a king who desires a queen, a slavemaster who desires a slave. She wanted there to be like two kings or two boys, no, it's better with two kings and then two kings and a servant and then another servant, then the king went into the monastery and the servants became monks, and they were drunk too, and the newest nun knew nothing of their intentions, no, she was completely naked in her cell, no, at the movies, right there, in the back row, in the bar, in the elevator, on the fifth floor, and the monks had a key to the hotel, and the queen was waiting for him there, she was waiting for the king, but in came three soldiers, into the hotel where the nun was, where the Swedish girl was, where the schoolgirl, the eighth-grader was, and she was innocent and the soldiers captured her and sold her to the slavemaster at the nightclub, aboard ship, on the train, and there was no one there, on the beach, and she swam in the nude while they watched her, those two foreigners watching the Swedish girl, and when she came out, no, yes, the second girl, when she went into the water, they were naked too, and she confessed, and he said that only a full confession would cleanse her soul, Father, and when only a little bit was left to go before the game was over, there was a shot, and this was at dawn on January 27. He killed him.

The river was utterly black against the white background of the snow, and the drops of blood were blue against the general bloody background. The man who was killed was Cricket, and he had been killed. At first it did not even matter who killed him; it mattered only that he was killed. And anyone could have been the killer but only someone who woke up at dawn, loaded his gun and fired a shot. A lot of people wake up at dawn, but not a lot load their guns, and fewer still fire shots. And if we don't count all those who did not wake up that morning, and if we then don't count those who didn't load their guns, and if we don't count those who did not fire any shots, then we would be left only with those who woke up, loaded and fired, and there would be two of them and only one who killed. But who? who are those two? and who is that one?

There was a sea of people at Cricket's funeral, and there was a sea of flowers and a sea of tears, and the coffin swayed as though riding the waves. He was killed for poetry, he was killed for writing poetry. For that and for nothing else. And the one who killed him could shit on poetry. He wanted to shit on poetry and on the one who wrote poetry. He killed him in the stomach.[20] But the one who killed the poet in the stomach for poetry still does not deserve the death penalty. And if the killer was a tsar, then he should be demoted to the rank of private, but what if the killer was a private? how do you demote him if he's already at the bottom. And what if the killer was a murderer, what if he was a professional, what if this was his profession: killing. Then one should not write poetry and one should not be a poet and one should not have a stomach that can be shot at. Any story has a history. The beginning of the story of the killing in Russia coincided with the beginning of the story of literature.

The story of literature began to develop after the story of the killing. The people were asleep and then suddenly woke up when the poet was killed. It's not like no one had ever killed a poet before, but after this killing they just started killing poets. It turns out that poets are the easiest of all to kill; they are mortal—it's their poetry that's immortal, while poets are just mortals. They started getting killed all over the place, and the killing really took off, just like in the first story of the killing. That is, at the end of the story it would turn out that it's not just that the poet is killed and that's it, but either he is killed in a duel or he is killed by thunder or by the sun or he was eaten or they even said that he killed himself, but this was not the case: after the first killing, as soon as it became clear that poets can be killed, they started killing them. And historically the story of literature developed with the story of the killing. And the more avant garde literature became, the more avant garde the killing became. Really, the classical killing corresponded to the classical period in literature. After this killing, there was even a live body left that still managed to say a live word before dying, while the most avant garde of killings left neither bodies nor words.

"Nicholas, most likely."

"More likely the dentist."

They started killing Cricket to see who can kill the most, and only the dentist could kill more than Nicholas, because he was more awake and he loaded more and he fired more. And, more than likely, he killed. More like wounded. More like Nicholas was the air that was difficult for Cricket to breathe in Nicholas's presence, and the dentist was more like the bullet that whistled through the air and struck Cricket, because bullets fly only in air that favors them. Most likely, that's not what happened. What happened was what happens when the landscape favors the eye: a bright sun, a clear sky without a single cloud to catch the eye, trees and shrubs strewn generously about, and a sea possessed of

85

sea waves and the sea smell, and all of this suddenly gives way to a landscape that favors the shot, namely: white snow, black trees, red blood. The fact that Cricket was in love with his wife and so was the dentist and so was Nicholas, and half of humankind could have fallen in love with her for she was so beautiful—all these facts taken together do not mean that she was so beautiful that a bullet should have killed Cricket. If Cricket's wife had been just as beautiful, and the dentist just as good a shot, and Cricket just as easily wounded, no one would have remembered the story of this killing, as no one remembers other stories of shots fired for love. Even if woman was the cause, the effect of Cricket's killing was still poetry.

And even if poetry was the cause, then in any case the effect of Cricket's killing was woman. That is, he would have been killed in either case—even if cause and effect had switched places. That is, this was the sort of case where he could not have been not killed. He would have been killed in any case—in case of war, in case of rain, in case of a lack of a suitable case. And what is frightening is not what happens but what cannot but happen. And when everything had drowned in this reality and reality drowned in itself, what was left was unreal, was what in reality could not be: Nicholas paid off Petia and Gleb O.R.'s debts because they had really accumulated a lot of debt while Gleb O.R. had power and while power had Gleb O.R., and Nicholas paid for them magnanimously, with a royal magnanimous gesture. He had not killed Cricket and had not demoted any tsars to the rank of private, because it was the dentist who killed him and then moved to a different city and lived there until death killed him, and what happened then was what happened before: if there was life before, then there was life then, and if there was death before, then there was death then. Whatever happens in this world is nothing new, and what is new is only what does not happen.

2

We are living in a time that has never before existed in the history of time, and we are witnessing a present unlike any that has ever come to pass, a present already living for the future. And the people, our contemporaries, are the sort of people of whom only a contemporary could say that he considers other contemporaries to be his contemporaries, that his contemporaries in spirit are not his contemporaries in time, that his contemporaries in spirit are those who came a bit earlier in time, at a time that has already been and passed, as opposed to the one that is. Everything is clear concerning those contemporaries who were contemporary to a past era, because they are dead, whereas those who are contemporary to the contemporary era are alive and nothing concerning them is clear.

That they are alive now does not mean they will be dead later. And the fact that they are living does not mean that they will die. What if they don't die? It happens. But what if it always happens but this time it won't happen? What if these contemporaries will forever go on being contemporary to the contemporary era?

But that is exactly what is going to happen. The beauty and horror of it all is that it will not be just one contemporary that dies but all the contemporaries together. There is not a single era that has left us a live contemporary. They are all dead, every single one, and their eras died with them. That is the way the eighteenth century died with all its contemporaries, and the nineteenth century with its contemporaries and the twentieth century with us. And by the end of the twenty-first century the twentieth century will become completely extinct: there will be not a single contemporary, not a single genius, not a single retard, they will all die, every single one, every eyewitness, and there will not be a single eyewitness left to remember what money was like in the twentieth century, what the wine was like, what the girls were like and the monsters and the masters, how they got with it, how they hanged, how they caught some rays, how they went to work, what kind of dudes they were, what kind of wheels they had, what kind of getups, what highs and bummers, how they raced, loved, grooved, wrote, read and drew—anyway, the sun will rise soon.

As much as the republic seceded, it rejoined, as much as people didn't go to work, they did, as much as they declared a hunger strike, they stopped it, inasmuch as a person can no longer be sold but he can be bought.

As many dictators have had power as have bad poets. But if a good poet comes to power, what if he becomes a good dictator— but this has never happened yet, good poets have never had power but bad poets have, such as Nero or Mao Tse-tung.

In no corner of the land has the land changed so drastically before. Only on our land can you take a walk on the bottom of the sea, or take a look at a sea fleet in the desert. When we construct canals we do it not for the sake of water but for the sake of geometry because there is a theorem that holds that parallel canals never cross, and that is the right answer. While everyone is nurturing grape arbors, we are chopping them down, while people live everywhere, our people become extinct; so everywhere life goes on while here life rages. After the republic rejoined, it turned out it was meant for vacation, that it was a resort where thousands of people came to better their health, which had gone bad at home, in their own republics, with breakfast, lunch and dinner, and a salmonella-free egg: proteins, egg yolk and tea. Construction cranes stand across the way. It's clear why they make so many construction cranes so that they stand at every site, giant against the clear blue sky, Magritte-like. And isn't it crazy when a crazy sort of love occurs against the background of a general craziness, as part of the craziness, and when general craziness happens against the background of this crazy love. After the republic rejoined, Gleb O.R. lost his power, that is, he lost his job. And Petia and Gleb O.R. were not allowed to stay in the same hotel room because they were not husband and wife, but if they had been father and daughter, they would have, and if they had been brother and sister, they would have; perhaps it would have been easier just to go ahead and get married but it would be even easier to adopt, so she adopted him and he adopted her, and as a result she was his sister and he her brother, and when their documents were completely legal, indicating that she was his mother and he her father, when their registration was in order, indicating that she was registered to live at his place and he at hers, which therefore meant that they were registered in the same place at the same time, and time here was only an hour behind. They bought the last of the wine, the wine of death, because it came from the grape arbors that had been chopped to death.[21] There was a strike. When public transportation doesn't function, taxis do. You can't buy wine at the store but you may buy it at the restaurant for more money. And life is the same except it's more expensive. This is the perfect place for staying in one place. You may, but you can't. We may go but we can't go. We may even buy, but we can't even do that. We may go to the market, but the market has been shut down. We may go on foot but only to the nearest corner. So we are left to stay and stew, but we can go swimming. But a stray bullet may stray or a knife may jump out of the water. It cannot. Can, too. And the land that stretches up to the horizon is free, but it is occupied like the night. We may go into town, but what if we are killed; if I am killed, you will bury me, and if you are killed, I will bury you, but what if we are wounded, what if they cut off our arms or legs and we are crippled—this can't happen but what will happen will be the sun, once daily, and the moon, once nightly, the moon that starts moving backward in the middle of the night, and we'll go to town while the sea is rolling and the sun is shining and he is— ellipsis. There is a writer in every room or a writer's wife, or a writer's son or a writer's daughter, or husband and wife, writers both. There are more writers per capita here than there are peasants, fishermen and hunters. And if all the writers were realists and described the absurdity around them realistically, then we would still end up with a literature of the absurd. But the more absurd life became, the more they chose for their literature a life that was totally un-lifelike, and in their writing construction advanced, fruit ripened and fishermen fished—that is, the acting subjects corresponded perfectly to their actions while the writers rested—while in reality you should eat well before lunch. Fish is fed chicken, and chicken is fed fish, and chicken smells fishy, and fish smells chickeny, and butter smells of oil. And black caviar may be edible but it cannot produce offspring, because it is artificial. Mass media are as heavy as mass transportation, and you can't get far using them.

The nice minister of the interior on television told the same little lies as the shop manager or the bus dispatcher. You couldn't really tell whether he conveyed so little information because his Russian was so poor or was it that his Russian was so poor because he had so little information to convey. Regarding unrest in the republic: "We drove through and we saw no mob scenes. We flew over and saw that there were no mob scenes any... We swam by..." Now this is poetry.

The plumbing has ruptured and now a little souvenir from Sochi is coming our way. We have degenerated to the extent that we may not regenerate. Here is an arithmetic problem for you: to put one man named Joseph in prison,[22] you had to get the tsar's signature, but to put half the population in prison all you needed was a single stroke of Joseph's pen, which would seem to mean that under the tsar the state was attentive to individuals while under the Soviets the state was attentive to the entire nation.

Now this is chemistry. If Petia and Gleb O.R. could not share a hotel room, they were allowed to share a table. They came together again. There was another person who shared their table, but they never saw this person in person. Meals were brought for this person, but the person never showed, so the meals stayed. You could even suppose that the meals were intended as a sacrifice to some pagan god who never touched them. Then one morning at breakfast—actually, there was soup on the table, which meant it was lunch, and there was yogurt, which meant it was supper—who should occupy this falsely set place but False Dmitri.[23] No one had seated him there. Passing himself off as Dmitri, he imposed himself on the seat, as an impostor. His looks were deceiving. Nothing about his looks betrayed the fact that these were his looks. He clearly wanted to resemble Dmitri, and less-observant people might even have taken him for Dmitri, but when he introduced himself, looking closely at Petia, when he said "Dmitri" and turned red, Petia and Gleb O.R. knew instantly that this was False Dmitri. As an impostor, he immediately went to work conquering their hearts. Where is the place for them? Why in Australia? because they are educated Europeans under thirty. Then why isn't it possible even for a twentysomething educated European to live under socialism, because life under socialism is impossible. "But don't order us around! Just don't!"—"How many people have we got altogether?"—"Two hundred-odd million."—"And how many of them live well?"—"umpteen million who belong to the *nomenklatura.*" The percentage of people who live well isn't high enough to make you want to revolt against them; what's so bad? that so many live well or that so many live poorly? A Russian beauty can make a Swede happy, and she won't do too badly if she marries him, but why should a Swede do so badly as to marry a Russian beauty when Russian beauties are all hard-currency prostitutes, though there they become good wives—the things you can drive a Russian beauty to do! The things you can drive Swedes to do—their Swedish hearts have been crushed the way the Swedes were crushed at Poltava, but Poltava is just a place, but the area of the heart is also a place. It took thousands of years to understand what kind of apple Adam and Eve ate. They ate fruit that at the end of the twentieth century was literally poisoned. What's wrong with it—nitrates and preservatives—nitrates won't kill you, but they might kick you out of Eden, that's all, and they did. We live in hell, literally, collective hell. Ants live under a totalitarian regime, so they are fascists, or they are Egyptians because they build pyramids; and people live under socialism, capitalism and imbecilism, where they have mosquitoes for murals. People stand before the closed grilles of a shop, and they are in prison, and when the shop opens, they will taste freedom. One always swims diagonally and walks at a right angle, so the diagonal is swimming, and the right angle is dry land.

False Dmitri was half falsehood: he was False Demi-tri. What Dmitri was he passing himself off as—a Dmitri that he was half of? This remained a mystery. And one of his halves negated the other, and in this respect he was human: he half-consisted of two halves. He was symmetrical. He had one head, but it had two eyes and one nose with two nostrils. He had two arms and walked on two legs; he was perfection incarnate, this half-False-demi-tri. As he was waiting for his wife (whom he called Tatya-Nyvanna and who had a dream on the eve of their wedding, just like Pushkin's Tanya did, complete with the snow and the bear and the handgun, and it's a good thing that Tanya did not marry Onegin, because he would have lied to her, but Tatya-Nyvanna did, and he did), three times he went into the shop that was shut for lunch from breakfast until dinner and asked for wine at the back door and was told, "We've got no wine."

"What kind of wine haven't you got?"

"We haven't got Alazan Valley."

"How much?"

"Five." No, what was surprising was not that they did not have it for three but that they did have it for five: they have chopped down all the grape arbors but there is still wine, like when a person has died but he is still alive. But the fact that Tatya-Nyvanna was a beauty and a Russian one at that and that she did not marry a Swede but married False Dmitri speaks to the fact that this is Moscow speaking, the time in Moscow is six o'clock in the morning, followed by the national anthem.

We are talking about something else entirely. But we should be talking about something else. We should make declarations of love but in such a way that no one will know. We should do it in writing. And you would write your note saying that you love me more than anyone or anything. And I will write that I love you, and then we will both write how we love each other together, in detail so that it is clear to whoever is going to read it how we love each other so. Not so easy. And we will submit our notes to the Central Literary Archives. And after we die, no, after twenty years, no, after a hundred years, after everyone who could get jealous of that description is dead, let them open those notes. And they will see that there is nothing unusual about it: we love each other the way people do, the way people know how, people know—which way? And there are migrant birds on the curtains and flowers and a bottomless pit of feeling, and all of this is in one room with the king and the queen, the six and the seven and the seventh trick, which must be won or you lose, and all of this is in one room where anything is possible except flight, but couldn't we just take flight, no, could we take flight and fly away, no, could we take flight, fly away and land and take flight again, is it possible that we are going to die? That's impossible to believe because it is utterly impossible to believe that. If this is a sociable sort of activity, this thinking of death and of paintings, then we are all at a big party, and what does dead mean—it means life is gone, but where has it gone to? it couldn't have gone nowhere, which means it must have gone somewhere, and where is that somewhere? far away! It has gone away far away. And if the dead one jumps up and runs after it, then he will catch it in a far-away place if he flies after it, if he swims after it, but if he walks after it, then he will not catch it, and if he just lies there dead, he will miss his chance and it will be the death of him, but it seems improper to go running after one's own life, so no Englishman and no Frenchman and no Russian will ever go running after it, because to do so would be improper and it would be more proper to die.

In the beginning was the rain. And the rain was everything. And then it was raining from the beginning at the end. And all that was left of the Tsar's Russia was the weather: the gray little rain, the clouds and the snow in winter. But there weren't any more of those royal snowbanks; for all that the tsar's regime under the Romanovs collected them, the new regime, with its greenhouse effect, shoveled them aside. There was almost no snow left. And as soon as the snow fell it would melt. And if it does not fall on its own, it will be fallen and then it will be melted. People can't just get away with doing this sort of violence to nature. Because people are as fickle as the weather, and if people can't survive on their own, they will be survived and then they will be extinct. The fact is that we live in the passive voice, that we are walked, we are addressed on the radio, and then we are cast away. And if we don't want to be cast away, we should stand firm, we should take a firmer stand, but even so they'll still stand to cast us off. Still, though, we are not lived but we live, because we are inspired by those who lived and survived in the active voice, like Nikolai Stepanovich.[24] If I may address you with this request, in writing or in person, or by telephone or through friends, or by way of the rain or in any way, Nikolai Stepanovich, if I may say so: you are loved, you are still loved as few who are alive today are loved, you are beloved, and some people have even hung up your photograph, the one with you wearing your officer's uniform and you are with your wife and your young son, and last year they finally published your poems so that now everyone who knew them is now reading them along with everyone who didn't, and if I may ask—this may seem a little strange, but I hope you do answer: Are you still alive even if you have been killed? or are you just the opposite—dead? because if you did not die a natural death, then naturally your heart did not stop of its own accord, which means that the force with which it pumped blood with such a terrific force, that force is still somewhere—but where, Nikolai Stepanovich? Maybe you can just say yes or no. Let's say that if you are alive, then if, let's say, it starts raining tomorrow exactly at noon, then you are alive, and if it doesn't, then you are not. We shall leave it up to the weather then, except let's not listen to the weather forecast for tomorrow, because this is an act of God and no one should know about it in advance. And there was something of God in the anchorman's voice when he started reading the weather for tomorrow and there was so much static on television that it got in the way of Petia and Gleb O.R. hearing the weather forecast for tomorrow. Though static was not the only thing that got in their way: the particular thing about Petia's room was that everything had to be done in a particular way. Take the water faucet, for instance. The cold water had to be turned off by turning the tap to a certain point of resistance but because water continued to come out in a tiny stream like Chinese water torture, you had to perform a slight movement of one finger, as in Tchaikovsky's *Swan Lake* ballet and at that moment water would give way to the divine sound of silence, but if you failed in that movement and the tap went a tiny bit too far, then water would come gushing out from the faucet with incredible force and it would have to be turned off all over again; also, in order to close the door, you had to raise it slightly using your shoulder; also, to turn on the light you had to pull on the string twice and the third time you had to stretch the string and hold it a bit; and also you had to be careful to walk around an entire lawn of squeaky parquet, but what kind of lawn is that? and if you did not turn a bit, hold a bit and raise a bit, then the object would refuse to perform the function it was intended for from birth, from childhood, and why do we have to sit on the toilet in such a way that it doesn't rock, because our toilet has not been born yet and it is still a fetus and Russia is full of black holes gaping all over, plus the electrification of the entire country.[25]

They missed it. They slept through it. They did not see whether he was alive or dead, whether it rained or not. Seems like it did; seems he is alive. It's better not to know.

The decorative nature of Caucasian shrubbery framed by love, or love framed by decorative shrubs is so wonderful that no one can tell you it is improper to kiss in such a proper place. Whereas the shrubbery of Middle Russia would truly not be the right decor, so kissing there would not be esthetically pleasing and would therefore be improper. In addition, the grass in the Caucasus is unusually tall, more suitable for prehistoric animals (such as people?), and the name of this prehistoric grass is bamboo. And at the bottom of the bamboo people with their undisguised kissing become utterly small and defenseless.

But we are not going anywhere, not anywhere—not away from the shrubs and not away from the shrubbery, not to any savanna or any prairie or any jungle, and even if our local conditions are unsuitable for living, no one can take away our conditions suitable for dying, no matter what the umpteen million are doing to create the conditions most ideally suitable for our departure because it's not the right place for us, it's not the right time, we don't act right—and we are not going anywhere no matter how much they may want it, even if it's worse than here because that's still better than better than there.

Tatya-Nyvanna was a magical sort of beauty: her face could change as though by magic and only occasionally did it take on a red color that was not beautiful, because it was not a blush that lit up her cheeks but the red of anger. And as if by magic, False Dmitri did not notice how beautiful Tatya-Nyvanna was. Her face was possessed of a golden section and the ratio of her features to one another was three to five, so her face was gathered at the nose and dispersed toward the hair. Her truthful eyes were so honest and her honest mouth was so truthful that, honestly, her face truly struck no false notes. And False Dmitri hated her especially when she was especially beautiful. She spoke little and, moreover, she did not much like it when others spoke more, and she had little use for what they said.

This was an uncommon sort of day, that is, it was the uncommon sort of morning that can transform into a day of uncommon beauty: a sea of uncommon beauty together with a few uncommon sun rays were breaking through uncommonly light clouds, and the uncommon kinds of trees that are common at this latitude along the longitude of the roads. Funny.

Petia and Gleb O.R. and Tatya-Nyvanna and False Dmitri sat at the table finishing their meal: Petia was finishing her compote while False Dmitri was still finishing his soup and Tatya-Nyvanna, who hadn't finished her second course, was just starting on the soup, which had just finished cooling, while Gleb O.R., who hadn't finished his appetizer but had finished all of his soup, was starting on the second course, and while he was eating it, Petia was washing it down with compote. The thought that came to Petia during lunch had totally poisoned the lunch for her. The thought was not a thought even but an unthinkable sort of excitement that engulfed her and may, in fact, be called thoughtlessness, but it seemed to her that the only reason she did not want to stop loving Gleb O.R. was that she did not love him. Because in order to stop loving you had to love and in order to want to stop loving you had to want to love, and in order to not want to stop loving you had to want to love. And thoughtlessly she thought that in fact she wanted to love but did not love, that to want to love and to love were two completely different things. And she said, "I don't" when Gleb O.R. asked her if she wanted his compote.

And what started then can in no way be explained except in the most thoughtless of ways.

Entered a young man who was remarkably ugly in a strangely beautiful way and, instantly choosing a rival, rapidly walked up to him. His rival was a bit on the fat side and a bit on the bald side but unusually agile. And when they stood opposite each other, face to face, something flitted between their faces like a stray bird, and it was a slap, which, as sure as the dawn will come, would surely be followed by a duel.

These two rivals had no contemporaries in the contemporary

95

world, so this story might have seemed old-fashioned to our con-temporaries had the duel ended one of their lives. But Nikolai Stepanovich's life ended in a death of a more avant garde sort, leaving the duel behind. Not even a body was left from his life after his death—not even a lifeless body, not even one momentar-ily killed by a bullet—and not even a place was left where his body could have been left in peace, so there was neither body nor place in the avant garde. But the most avant garde part of this killing was that although Nikolai Stepanovich was killed, he died of natural causes; that is, he was the last person in that story to die for his own causes—he was the last hero in his story who died in time to die as he had lived, whereas after his most avant garde of deaths came the sort of death that killed people before they died, so that they died while they were still alive and they survived when already dead. But he survived! no matter that there was a change of sex and women became men and men became women, that there was a change of direction and though the sun rose in the east and set in the west, it warmed rivers that flowed back-wards, and that there were other changes, and that good was ex-changed for evil and everything for everything else, because the human being's functions remained the same: he ate, slept, woke up and made love to the sound of *Carmen* the opera, though who knows what sounds Carmen herself made love to.

The nightmare began at the height of the season and lasted through the fall, when seasonal birds had emigrated and seasonal wear had immigrated. The nightmare was lit by the rays of the burning sun as well as the setting sun and the sun rising the fol-lowing morning.

Better not to swim at all than to have to go swimming in a bul-letproof vest—better to swim in the nude. Petia and False Dmitri had a chance meeting underwater after their feet had had a chance meeting under the table the day before. No one noticed their innocent touch under the table, the same as underwater. This way their affair got under way. Not just three times a day, during their intake of food, but more frequently, when Petia went to the market, when Gleb O.R. napped and when False Dmitri managed to fool Tatya-Nyvanna. After their first underwa-ter meeting Petia decided that there could be no second meeting, not underwater, not underground, not under any pretense, no way, but then in spite of it all and contrary to and apart from it all, it happened. It happened at night, when Petia ostensibly stayed in her room, after telling Gleb O.R. that she had a headache and stayed in under that pretense, while False Dmitri ostensibly stayed in a nearby town under the pretense that there was ostensibly no transportation, they met in the moonlight. How absurd it is to be building a love within the framework of marriage, and how absurd it is to be building capitalism within the framework of socialism. Joint ventures, joint-stock holdings, farmers who don't own their land are all like double adulterers. Just say no to marriage and throw yourself into love; just say no to socialism and throw yourself into capitalism. It's hard to say no. Not very easy at all. Not that anyone is going to let us. We are monitored by husband and wife and umpteen million members of the *nomenklatura*. Though Petia worried about this more than False Dmitri did.

"Why should you worry when you are not married?" False Dmitri entreated her.

That was exactly the point. She should have married Gleb O.R. first so that she could then have divorced him, and that way it would have been honest: she should have stopped loving Gleb O.R. so that then she could love someone else, even someone like False Dmitri, but Petia did not want to stop loving, so better to let it be dishonest, better to let it be worse, better this sort of life than a military coup, a life that's bad for you is still better than a good death. Or else we could just do it all at once, with no shots and no blood, just poison the earth and let the atmosphere go into space, poison the heart and let the soul go. All at once.

"I'll get a divorce," said False Dmitri because he was already married and consequently he did not have to marry Tatya-Nyvanna first in order to divorce her later.

"That we could do without." But could we do without noting that the hour they spent together, which they could have gone without, was not without charm? In their swim suits, without their swim suits, underwater, by the water, by the moon, under the moon.

The location of the Lord's heavenly kingdom is this, the gray of the morning when the local sky where the sun is slated to appear—that location in the sky where it will appear is already pink but there is no sun yet. When you are naked in the water, then the idea of the male and female sexes as such seems shallow compared to the depth of the sea. And it seems that here is another unrealized human ability: if people were capable of living under water, they would be cleaner, not in the sense of cleanliness but in the sense of depth—maybe it only seems like this as long as you don't have to eat or sleep, but could it be that this light body that is so light in the water is the same body that can barely walk on the ground wearing high heels. Perhaps the androgyne is a sea animal: people became men and women on dry land, but in the water men and women are people. And this androgyne—this person, that is—had two backs, two bums and two backs of the head, meaning that he was man and woman on the inside, or was it the other way around and he was man and woman on the outside and broke apart along the back? or was he a mutually penetrating person, meaning that if a man and a woman are placed face to face and fused together and if they have the ability to pass through bodies then the woman will end up behind the man's back the same way that after the man passes through the woman he will end up behind her back. And if they are placed back to back, once again retaining that ability to pass through bodies, then when they have passed through each other they will once again end up face to face, so is this what an androgyne is? or is it a person? The Soviet person is face to face with the hostility of milk and meat, which, according to anti-Soviet writing, he can't get, but he actually can't get them, and according to anti-Soviet writing the rivers and the Kazakhs are dying, but they actually are dying along with the Tungus, then why is this life called Soviet and that writing is called anti-Soviet? because you are not allowed to write about it, you are only allowed to live it, and the *nomenklatura,* which steals in anti-Soviet writing, but then it actually does steal in Soviet life, which means that the *nomenklatura* leads an anti-Soviet life. While we lead Soviet lives. Except it is difficult for a Soviet person to lead a Soviet life: to buy and not to steal. There is nothing to buy and it is bad to steal. But how can this be! can this be! but! this! be! but we will collapse like Rome—we have already collapsed—but Rome left us the Capitoline, and what will we leave to us—concrete-block towers as well as maybe some of the things that Russia left us: streets, churches, trees and houses, though there are no more streets left. And it is not easy to live in a country where all the power is in the hands of the people, and anyway, power has driven people to the point where their labor has started to seem meaningless: why plant if we'll have to throw it out anyway, and why live if we'll have to die anyway. Labor is completely unprofitable, as is life, and the food is bad for you

98

and so is life. That leaves just the heavenly side of things, which makes life worth living, and that is: weather—rain, snow and the wind; stars at night and the sun in the morning; and autumn trees with springtime buds and winter streams of snowy water; and endless forests with a few trees; and the marvelous birds with their hoarse voices; and family dogs with lonely owners; and pregnant cats with childless girls, and everything else in life for which the soul yearns, which the materialists negate because it's all gone to their heads. So if they are going to insist on negating it, that means they don't have souls, but we do, and that's all there is to it! and here's to all our soul mates, who've got souls, too. But maybe our suffering is as it should be. And Pushkin was anti-Soviet under the tsar, and so was Dostoevsky, and the Decembrists were nabbed by the cops. It's a good thing that in Australia life is good and writing is bad, or is it bad that here life is bad but writing is good? Hail to the bad life for the sake of good writing and have no pity for the poet who lives poor but writes well. But it's too bad about the people who don't write anything but have bad lives. What is the point of their suffering, which takes place not in their writing but in real life? so they can be live characters in lively writing? Boo-hoo! Thank you to all the Russian peasants who suffered for the sake of Pushkin's good writing! boo-hoo! Thank you to all the Soviet people who suffer for the sake of the Soviet writer's good writing. And shame on all the Soviet writers who write poorly while the Soviet people suffer for their writing, because it is not so shameful to write poorly in Australia, since the people live well there, but it is shameful to write poorly here because the people live poorly here, because boo-hoo.

In these artificial conditions created for artificial living, some things were still real but communication was artificial because a commonality created artificially did not want to be common but wanted to be human (woman and man), familial (mommy and daddy) or national (French, American, Tartar). False Dmitri was looking off into the distance waiting for Petia. He kept looking and she kept not coming. The advantages of this place (where he was waiting for her) were determined by its disadvantages. All these advantages would have been too much for any other place, but for this place even all these disadvantages were not enough.

The great thing known as asymmetry, of which only nature is capable, was present here in every cell of live tissue. If one tree craned to one side, then another craned to the opposite side. If a number of clouds on one side of the sky were a bit higher, then it looked like the clouds on the other side of the sky were a bit lower—and did not look at all like clouds. And irregular lines of forest cut through the rows of mountains, and they were joined by pasture fields the shapes of which were distorted by perspective. Even the most ordinary electrical lines added something special to this picture of asymmetry because their endlessly long length underscored the irregularity of the landscape. And all the width far and wide and all the length far and long were kind to the eye and the eye feasted on them.

After supper, but not yet finished with it, False Dmitri waited for Petia and, but not yet waiting long enough for the sun to set while he was sitting there, he started walking along the beach waiting for the moon to come out while he was walking. The most miraculous thing was that (though miracles do not happen) Gleb O.R. never asked Petia where she had been after she had not been with him. Once not letting her tell an honest lie, stopping her halfway to telling him where she had been when she had not been with him, he let her know that it was not that he didn't really care whether he knew where she had really been but that he really cared not to know where she had really been. And he was magnificent in his desire to not know. As much as she wanted to love him, he did not want to know that she wanted to.

Petia saw False Dmitri when he was just standing there taking a look at the sea. He was not taking in the sea and he was not losing himself in the sea; he was looking at the sea as though it were a highway and a car were due to come around the bend on the horizon. And when he saw Petia and saw that she had seen him looking at the sea and when he saw that she had seen something unappealing in his outlook, he made it look like he had not seen her. And only when she came right up to him did he look like he had just seen her. He had an amazing ability to lie. After lying to Tatya-Nyvanna and telling her that he was going off to the airport to pick up a friend (this lie was perfection itself in that it covered both a long and a short time period, since he could either pick up his friend quickly and come right back or the flight could be late and he could only come back by morning, as necessary), he lied to Petia, telling her that Tatya-Nyvanna had gone to the airport to pick up a friend and he was now completely free. He even suggested something incredible: that they go over to his place. Petia said, "yes, well, nah," and they started to walk along the beach. The beach was something like a road: they went where it led them. So they walked and walked while all around them it got darker and darker until it got dark. And before they got to a big cluster of lights, they turned onto a road where there were not many lights and the lights that were there were dim and distorted the street with their light more than they illuminated it. Really, having been on this street during the day, in daylight, False Dmitri had noticed this one building, but he was having a hard time finding it in this artificial light.

"Maybe it's this one."

"What are you looking for?" asked Petia.

They stood in front of a long one-story building that stretched into the night the way a train stretches into the distance. There were lights on in some of the windows, and False Dmitri was looking for a window.

"Maybe it's this one."

"Who are you looking for?" asked Petia.

He knocked on a dimly lit window and the light immediately went off and then someone opened the window from the inside.

"Climb in," False Dmitri said to Petia.

"Where?"

"I'll give you a hand."

He lifted her up and set her down on the windowsill. He climbed in after her, and together they jumped down into the dark room. He found a light switch and turned on a lamp. There was nothing (and no one) special about the room. There was hardly any furniture and hardly any sign of life aside from an un-finished glass of tea.

"Exotic," said Petia. She pretty much expected that now might be the time for it to happen. But it was not happening. False Dmitri walked around the room calmly, and as he paced she sat, and he finished off the tea and closed the window. It was still not happening, and Petia was thinking, "I wish it were over already."

And when False Dmitri came up to her from behind and took her by the shoulders, she thought, "Now it's happening." But what was happening was not it, but what had already happened once under entirely different circumstances. But what was hap-pening was exactly what was happening. And it was happening naturally, in a way. Petia heard someone on the other side of the wall reciting poetry. And at first they were reciting kind of quietly so that you could only tell by the rhythm of it that it was poetry and not just a regular conversation. And Petia asked, "Is this a dorm?"

"Maybe it is."

"These rooms," Petia said, "are like cells."

She went up to the window and looked out into the garden.

"Maybe it's a jail?"

"Maybe it is," said False Dmitri, "a garden jail."

And then the poetry reading on the other side of the wall got louder. And louder and louder. And now you could hear every word.

"Whose poetry is this?" asked Petia.

"Don't you recognize it?"

The poetry and the voice really belonged to Nikolai Stepanovich. And when he finished reading his poetry, someone else would start speaking, and this someone was, of course, someone whose name has been preserved by history, but since it has been so well-preserved, we shall not name this other person, because the killer could have gone by any name, and the name could have gone to any killer, but the poet who was reading his poetry could only have gone by one name, and that name is Nikolai Stepanovich.

During the breaks in the reading the poet and the killer were having a perfectly peaceful conversation, a friendly chat. One would have to be a major killer to be able to have a friendly chat and then commit a friendly killing. And there came a moment when everything went quiet. The word and everything. And you couldn't even hear the shot on the other side of the wall, because this kind of jail had a kind of cellar where they kind of took people and killed them. One moment they were just shooting at a person who was alive, and in a moment he became a dead person. And this moment was an eternity. And we know perfectly well that all of them, you know, were shot and buried we don't know where. We don't know at all. We know only that it was not by this sea but by that one, and not this year but that year, and not under this sun but under that one, and not this August but that one, but we don't know on what day. And it started to rain. And as soon as it started to rain, a solid wall of rain cut the window off from the garden and the sea, and everything that was behind the wall of the rain was that side of the rain and everything that was in front of the rain was this side of evil. Petia and False

Dmitri jumped out the window and went through the wall of rain and ran, and the farther they ran away from the rain, the less rain there was because it was clearly occurring not in time but in space. And it was finished completely when they finished running through the space to which it extended. And it would have been good if the sun had come out, but the moon came out instead, and instead of drying their clothes, it enveloped them in such a chill that they got really cold. It may have been the moon. When they walked up to the building, there was activity only on one side, where the door was open.

Petia said:

"All right, I'm going."

"Wait," he said. "Don't go."

"I've got somebody waiting," she said. "All right."

Petia went up to the elevator, and while the elevator was coming down, False Dmitri was looking down at her and she was looking up at him, and she said, "All right, see you tomorrow."

"Wait," he said. "You know what—"

The elevator doors opened. "What?" said Petia. "Go on."

And False Dmitri stepped into the elevator, and Petia walked toward the stairs, but False Dmitri managed to jump out of the elevator and catch up to her by the stairs.

"Don't go now," he said.

She walked up to her floor, and though this wasn't his floor, he followed her down the hall. She opened the door to her room, and False Dmitri entered it as though it had been his own. He took off his clothes, which were completely wet, and got under the blanket.

"Come here," he said.

His simple ways were simply magnificent, and he got to her. Is that not the commandment for our time: "Thou shall not get to others lest you be gotten to"? He'd get her to come here. He'd get her to stand there. He'd get her to sit down. He'd get her to lie down. She continued to stand: get not and you shall not be gotten, do not get to others and others shall not get to you, do not get to her and she shall not get to you, do not get to them and they shall not get to you, do not get to us and we shall not get to you. But they'll get you anyway! they'll get you no matter what, no matter what it takes to get you. They will get you and they will... they'll get and they will... you get and you will... you will be gotten, do not kill but you will be killed, do not rob but you will

103

be robbed, do not love but you will be loved, do love and you will not be loved. But if you do not get to others, you will not be gotten to.

It would have been easiest to do the hardest thing, to make it all into a joke and have a laugh together. Funny. Not funny at all. Angelic laughter, heavenly laughter, a gurgling in the chest, laughter that cleanses and infuses with life, laughter through tears is not funny. The fact that Petia was standing, False Dmitri was lying, the moon was shining, the sea was glistening, the sun was not, and Nikolai Stepanovich was dead—all of this made no sense.

Why was Petia like Poor Liza but did not drown herself; like Pushkin's Tanya but did not marry another; like Anna Karenina but did not throw herself under a train?[26] Because because.

"Let's see each other tomorrow," Petia said to False Dmitri. "Now you go."

"You are lying," said False Dmitri.

And Petia couldn't say anything to that because she really was lying.

"I want to understand you," said False Dmitri.

"I want you to leave."

"And then what?"

"That's it."

"Why?"

"Because."

And there was nothing else to talk about. All the regular and irregular verbs, all the participles, all the long dashes, all the syntax and all that jazz had gotten to her. And False Dmitri, he could get her anywhere now—in the air, on a train or on screen, in movement, in flight or in stasis, in any conversation. The mechanism of getting to her was primitive: you say "yes," you say "no," you say "no," you say "yes." That's it. That's the mechanism. How simple. We'll go, we won't go, black, white, come in, go out. If you say "I would rather die," he'll say, "I would rather live," if you say, "Live, then," he'll say, "I'm going to die." Here we are.

"Listen," said Petia. "Get out of here!" It was rude. But she could not get through to him any other way. He was livid and he was naked. And a naked human being who is livid is quite defenseless. Like an animal in shock. No, more shocking than that. Like a human monster. No, more monstrous than that. Like a disarmed monster with two fists in his forehead. And there is no way out but the door and the window. Or a commandment if it had been observed: "Thou shall not get to others, lest you be gotten to."

He got dressed, said a prayer, had some food, had a nap, had a drink and said, "You don't like me. Why did you come? I mean yesterday, to see me."

"I'm sorry," said Petia. "I don't even know."

"But I know," said False Dmitri. "You will never ever love anyone. You are doomed to unhappiness."

There was nothing particularly happy about standing next to a person who was alive and sad and an unhappy person. If he had been happy, he would have left. He was unhappy and he was not leaving. And she couldn't make him happy.

"Well, be happy," said Petia and opened the door for him.

So he left and he did not say anything, and therefore he did not tell a lie. For the first time. Heavenly False-demi-tri, half heavenly. The episode was over. It was time to go to sleep. And if life consisted of episodes instead of life, then it was definitely time to go to sleep. All together now. Bon voyage! See you in our dreams!

This way, by letting her body parts go swim through the parts of the world or in parts of the world ocean, getting a tan and a rest this way, getting some sleep and her strength back, Petia and Gleb O.R. gathered their wits about them and started gathering their stuff to go home, to their one and only, their dear, their most beautiful, magnificent and favorite Muscovy. And if all the republics secede, if they migrate like migrant birds, then the only one that won't migrate will be Muscovy. And even if Great Novgorod migrates to the north, and if Kievan Rus' migrates and the *Rzeczpospolita* and the Golden Horde migrate,[27] Moscow will still have its Muscovy. They say there's a sea near Moscow and they say you can go swimming there underground, and they say no mother turtle has ever seen her baby and no baby turtle has ever seen its mother, and for some reason a turtle egg is wiser than a human embryo, and for some reason a newborn turtle is smarter than a human newborn, but still man is the crown of creation, so why is that?

PART THREE

1

Who is that last person who has that last laugh, anyway? and the day was so gray with gray roses in the sky, the gray roses were clouds, which were gray-rose-colored... It was an accident that Petia was late for a business appointment, and by some accident she arrived right on time. Having promised to come exactly at one and having been exactly one hour late, she came exactly at one. But that cannot be. Can too, when there is daylight savings time and regular time so that in the summer we get up an hour early but in the winter we go to bed on time, so that we have more calories, so that we absorb more sunlight and store it up for the winter, so we have an hour in storage just like Europe—all of Europe has daylight savings time in the summer, and we are like Europe: we both don't have much sun and we both save time, and we are virtually European.[28]

Even though Petia's watch said it was two o'clock exactly, the clock in the square said it was exactly one o'clock. And just about beneath the clock, which was telling regular time, which was now advancing toward winter, in the middle of autumn, in that hour that no longer existed but that Petia happened to have saved, in that *summer* hour left over from *summer* time, Boris accidentally appeared. There may be a thousand explanations for this, but none of them can explain what an accidental meeting means and what accidents mean and what it means to meet but not by accident. Since there could have been no such time, then Petia could not have been in the square and the businessman could not have been there, since Petia was late; there could only have been the square itself and the time over it. And what we call an accident is that they met at that time that was over the square at that time. After she talked business with the businessman and forgot all about the business, which could be defined as follows: business is an action uncharacteristic of action and inaction, and he who can see, shall we say, action in inaction and inaction in action, is wise and that's that, and the ways of action are filled with darkness, and Petia put business aside and got down to love, which cannot be defined. It turned out that, as though by accident, Petia and Boris were headed in the same direction, and she took his arm so that they could cross the street underground when the light was red.

"You get prettier and prettier," said Boris, "every day."

They had loved each other when love, historically, did not love them, and they had separated; and we should think that they came together when love, historically, began to love them.

They lost their way and ended up at Boris's building, at his studio. There was a small staircase leading up from the quasi-basement, which indicated that Boris had become fantastically rich and one could now observe the street from above as well as from below, from the second floor as well as from the basement windows. Down at the bottom, amid boxes with his sculptures in them, stood a car, which he had brought from "over there," having traded a sculpture for it "over there." The car stood sculpture-like, but to make it funny, to make it into a composition, Boris turned on a traffic light in the corner of the room, and it started blinking, and when the light was green, Petia crossed the street, and they embraced. They were embracing for an endlessly long time, and at the end of this endlessness, after the end result had been achieved, at the end of the road at the end of the day, they talked, and it turned out that he loved her and she loved him and they loved he and they loved she and it loved it.

This person shall receive an inheritance from a relative abroad, and this inheritance will ensure her prosperity: jack of clubs, jack of hearts, jack of diamonds.

This person shall attract with her heart as well as with her mind: eight of spades, eight of hearts, eight of diamonds.

A friend's honesty will enable this person to see the envy of another friend, whom she has counted as her best friend until now, and it will help her to rid herself of this person once and for all: two of clubs, two of hearts, two of diamonds.

A light bulb shone in the fog, a candle flickered in the smog, and tears streamed down her legs, and there was a rose in repose, the soul hadn't yet departed, in fact it barely had parted from the body, life is a composition but life is also the stream of life. This poor room, a few steps wide, long as a long day, tall as big words: there is no room. By some miracle poverty had been preserved in the corner, an unusually poor design: instead of a painting on the wall, there was a nail where the painting used to hang; traces of glue on the wallpaper where a photograph had been glued, and a cross in the fog, and a coat in the smog, and what is there to say. Petia found the photograph that had come unglued and glued it on; she hung the painting that used to hang on that nail when Petia was last here, and in this corner of the room, if only in this

110

one, in this part of the world, in this corner of the soul, everything became as it was before, as if there had not been any separation. But separation was in every corner of every other corner. How nice it would be if it started snowing now, thought Petia, because that would bring back that state of when they separated when they loved each other when it was snowing when the shovel started scraping over her head as though she were being buried—and a miracle happened and it started snowing for the first time at the end of the summer, wet snow, rain, actually, but still snow because snow is lighter than rain and she felt lighter after that rainstorm and sad because it brought sadness.

Is it not happiness itself to go up the steps—to observe your own happiness from above? Their meeting was not entirely accidental, and life itself is an ordered sequence of accidents. The first accident is the accident of birth and the last accident is death. Nothing else is accidental.

No one except their biographers will ever know how Petia and Boris ended up out of town. How they got there (by bus, train or taxi?), what moved them to go (a telephone call, a telegram, a letter?), and on what date? actually, was there a date? how much time has passed since then, and has this time passed at all? For some reason, it was still fall. And the place where they were going was a place in the middle of time.

Maybe they were simply going to visit someone. Maybe. But not simply. Only once will the first letters of your first and last names be capitalized, as they should be—E.S.[29]—and hereinafter the capital letters will be replaced with lower-case ones—e.s.—because though more than anything else you are a person, though a dead one, but more than being a person you are a poet, but as the poet e.s. you died before you died as a person, and all the life there was left in you was an essential supply of life—e.s. Even if you were not killed as a person, the poet in you was killed in the person, and all that was left for you was e.s. They took away your soul, didn't they?

The conversation in the middle of which Petia and Boris entered the conversation, so they did not hear the beginning of the conversation, was vague: cigarette smoke was wafting up from the nighttime pastures, cows were following one another to their barn, the heart was at peace, but the conversation was not peaceful. The fact that one of the people speaking had a poetic appearance and the other an unpoetic appearance did not mean that

111

one of them was a poet and the other one was not.

What else could we tell about them right away? that one of them was a guest and the other was the host, and the guest addressed the host in a sort of ironically deferential way, an almost ironic way, calling him e.s. Even though he was addressing him orally and not in writing, his intonation indicated lower-case "e" and "s." How he managed even in a private conversation to indicate lower-case letters was a mystery. For his part, e.s. addressed him as "my dear." This "my dear" had rather pleasing and correct facial features, though it would be more correct to say that some of his pleasing features smoothed over his other, less pleasing features. On the other hand, e.s., though he was a bit short as well as a bit overweight and a bit bald, had something about him, something so simple, something so complex, and he had blue eyes and pink cheeks, and he sang. He spoke poorly but sang well. And he ate poorly and not much and drank too much. Whereas "my dear" ate well, drank and sang along well. They were probably having a good time together the two of them before Petia and Boris arrived. Boris was still the same poor Boris, except he was now rich. And when e.s. saw Petia, he said, "Well, what shall I sing for you, my dear?" And though e.s. was twice as old as Petia or maybe even older than that, Petia said, "Hey, whatever, sing something you like."

And when e.s. started singing, he turned into the most beautiful man in the room. Even though the most loved man in the room was Boris, e.s. was the most loved. For some reason, e.s. was crying. And the way he was crying was not the way of someone who is singing but the way of someone who is crying. The smoke of tears made him as difficult to see as a fire in a fog. His cheeks got red and his eyes got blue. When he was drunk he was not at all good-looking, and the good-looking rays of light from the table lamp streamed to the south and dissolved in the southern corner. While e.s. was singing, he spoke well, but when he stopped singing and started speaking, he spoke very poorly and this gravity did not come from age but from life, which has no age because it just has either gravity or levity. And it wasn't even because he was drunk. And through the tears and the fogged-up windows, beyond which you can't see anything, so if you push apart the trees that don't let you see far, then you will see a railroad station all lit up and half a river, a river chopped off, a cemetery littered with monuments with dead people underground in silence, and finally a certain concept will crystallize, which will have to be defined to be introduced; what is social mimicry? it is a disease that affects all Soviet people, that makes you want to cry when you look down at the street or up at a building, or inside a store or in the courtyards outside, so that wherever you look it makes you want to cry. This is a disease, of course. And e.s. said, "What's there to talk about: we'll be sick awhile and then we'll die." You could be sick awhile and get better or you could be sick awhile and die. "But who knows where we are?" asked "my dear." "We are all abroad," answered Petia.

"Is there no doubt about that?"

"There is no doubt about that we are abroad."

They were uninvited—that is, they had no letter of invitation to the suburb that was located not outside the city but outside the country, where there was a different country, though this country was located not in the next country but a few countries over, and across a sea border and then across and then there where the forest borders on the river, they went one after another, like in a race, a friendly race, a race of friends. As soon as Boris appeared in the room, Gleb O.R. appeared right after him. There was nothing surprising about False Dmitri's appearance, because he always knew how to get to people. And Tatya-Nyvanna appeared as his wife. And what about Yezdandukta? she appeared just as Petia's sister because after Boris spent a year loving her as a human being, he realized that it is inhumane to love a woman as a human being, so they separated, and they met again here. And as soon as everybody met, all of them abroad, all of them as free individuals rather than as repressed people in their home country, they all decided to send a letter home. This was a letter not to a private individual but to a person known all around the world, and, we should note, loved all around the world, the first Man of the Year,[30] if people really have such a concept as "person of the year," as though a person only happened once a year. This was not a letter from a bunch of crazies or from a hospital or from a jail; it was a letter written by normal people who were maybe no worse off than other people and maybe even better off, but then there were people who were even better off than that but did not think about those who were worse off, and this letter was from people who were like the Decembrists except they did not want the tsar to die, they just wanted to ask the First Person of the Year something they'd been afraid to ask back home but were

113

not afraid to ask abroad. Because a lot of different revolutionary ideas were originally expressed abroad and then they trickled down to the homeland. Herzen was preparing the revolution abroad, and it was he who awakened the Decembrists, and they acted it out at home. And Lenin, too, thought abroad and acted at home. The letter began as follows: "Dear Mikhail Sergeyevich..." Then there was a long passage concerning Pushkin and Nicholas meeting at the dance and the fact that what ultimately killed Pushkin was not the tsar's regime but the Petersburg air, which was poisoned by autocracy. And in the end the letter said that it is unfortunate that we live at this moment, the moment of Soviet rule, which is a mere moment in eternity, and that in the face of eternity no one will be able to tell people that at this moment they were happy, and no one can say, "Oh, moment, stay, you are so beautiful!"[31] unless it concerns the weather or the view because the weather can be beautiful anywhere the same as it can be horrible anywhere. The weather can be bad under capitalism, and this does not preclude the weather being good under socialism. The weather does not belong to people, people belong to the weather. The fact that all the friends ended up abroad was quite certain. This was a far-away place, clean and well looked-after, with clean earth underfoot and a clean sky overhead. The friends stepped outside to breathe some fresh air, and the air was fresh. And it was important that this was a country, but it was completely unimportant which country. This was basically "abroad," specifically abroad as opposed to at home. It could have been the south of France, but the northern wind was a bit cold and there were too many northern shrubs and there were too many northern birds that had migrated from the south for it to be the south of France. It was about time for introductions. Because before everyone came together abroad, virtually no one had ever seen each other.

—
—
—
—
—
—
—
—
—

114

—
—
—

So they all met. The more the merrier, the stronger the better, the closer than before, higher and higher, so they all settled down. Theirs was a small colony, like a colony of birds. There was a lot of noise and few words and a lot of singing: it was a living language. The house had two rooms suitable for living. They wisely decided to divide it into male and female halves. The women would all sleep together in one room, and all the men would sleep together in the other. And women would sleep on the second floor, and so men don't feel like they have been taken advantage of, they'll get the first floor. But so no one would feel taken advantage of, it turned out that the house had only one floor; it was a single-level house. But the building had two separate exits, and one door opened out onto the garden and the other also opened out onto the garden. After a filling supper came fulfilling sleep, and the feeling of comfort put them to sleep. Everything that had not been settled at night was settled in the morning. It turned out that the owner of the garden building was not e.s., who was still asleep, but "my dear," who was already waking up. When he finally woke up, he made a final decision to hold a reception and have a toast to the land on which the building was located and to the governor of the city, to whom the people of the city had entrusted their souls, and to the well-being of those souls, and it also occurred to him to invite the postmaster, in honor of the excellence of the local postal service... And in the

---

[1]*What is your name? (Eng.)*

[2]*Я живу в Москве.*

[3]*Comment vous appelez-vous?*

[4]*Ich habe 25 jahre.*

[5]*Wie heissen sie?*

[6]*Oui, I was born in Moscow.*

[7]*And where do you live?*

[8]*Mein Familienname ist–*

[9]*How are you?*

[10]*Ja, ich bin geboren*

[11]*Как вас зовут?*

[12]*Nicht verstehe.*

morning the landlord shared his ideas with e.s.: "Also I could invite the ambassador and his wife, the movie star with her brother, and the superintendent with his elderly mother."

"My dear," said e.s. "But what about our folk?" By "our folk" he meant Gleb O.R., Boris, Petia and her sister and the young married couple.

"But they are bohemians, this Petia and the rest of them with the sister and the couple. It would be unbecoming, so they could have an outing, take in the sights."

e.s. argued with him, but "my dear," who was actually the Dutch ambassador's stepson, had such a way with words that, without saying much, he managed to convince e.s. A lot of this had to do with his appearance. He was beautiful, and he could speak beautifully and even when he came across words that were not beautiful, he managed to insert them in such a way that instead of being painful to the ear they were almost kind to it. And after he was kind to e.s. with these words, of which there are only three such ugly words in the Russian language—but there are so many derivatives and related words—"my dear" finally killed him with kindness and won. And e.s. lost. And "my dear" won. And to show e.s. that he was especially disposed toward him, to make e.s. trust him like no one else, "my dear" told him that his stepfather was actually his stepbrother. "But can that be?" But soon e.s. would learn that anything can be. He ordered *hors d'oeuvres* and had wine brought in, and then my dear discovered that there was only enough silverware for six people in the house. But if there were more guests than there were forks, then it would be better that the quantity and quality of guests correspond to the quantity and quality of silverware. That took care of the governor and the postmaster. That left the movie star with her brother and the superintendent with his elderly mother. And when the table was already set for six, it turned out that the movie star's brother had suddenly died with the last rays of the setting sun. The same rays illuminated the table, which was beautiful: it had color, odor and depth, as well as texture and density. There were reflections as well as beautifully arranged specks of light. And though some things were out of order, everything else was in perfect order. Order up. "My dear," said e.s., "this is so beautiful." They were sitting next to each other and looking at the pitchers, which got smaller in perspective at the table end closest to the horizon while nearby plates got bigger. They were sitting and waiting, and

116

the superintendent kept not coming. They had to wait a long time until the doorbell rang. And when my dear went to open the door and asked "Who is there?" he heard, "Us."

Us was, in fact, them. They were the young couple—False Dmitri and his wife—and two sisters—Petia and Yezdandukta—and Gleb O.R., Boris, or Gleb or Boris. The total number of them was two forks more and two chairs short, and the young couple had to share a chair, and the two sisters also took just one chair. And after they had a drink and a bite to eat and, shall we say, a little rest, they remembered about the superintendent and his elderly mother. "If she is not dead yet," said my dear, "then I am going to marry her."

"A marriage of convenience?" asked Petia. "But you are so young and beautiful. And you are rich."

Looking from a distance—from abroad—it was easy to see how rich "abroad" was and how poor at home was. Home had riches in its bowels—its riches were underground—but there were no riches above ground; "abroad" was the other way around: there was virtually nothing of value underground, but everything that stood, sat or lay on the ground was treated as a thing of great value, and valuable houses stood in valuable gardens with valuable stars above them and valuable apples in the orchard.

"Life sure is expensive here."

"But life is man's most valuable possession."

"But at home life is cheap, and human life is cheap, and the people themselves are cheap."

"But I must say that the French are an amazing people. At home how many people speak French? I mean no one does, I mean hardly anyone does. But in France even street sweepers speak French, even cops do."

"But under the tsar people spoke French in Russia: the tsar did and the tsarina did, and Pushkin wrote in French, and the entire Third Duma spoke French: they thought in Russian and talked in French.[32] But what language does the government think in now? and what language does it speak?"

"It certainly isn't Russian!"

"Did anyone say that they think in Russian?"

"Did anyone say that they talk in Russian?"

"In America all the Americans live American: they all get paid in dollars and shop in hard-currency stores. Every single one of them and not just some of them, like some of us."

"If a girl fell in love with you and she was poor and beautiful," asked Petia, "could you fall in love with her?"

"That would depend on how poor and how beautiful she was," my dear responded after some consideration.

"What if she were absolutely poor and absolutely beautiful?"

"And she loved me absolutely? What kind of question is that?" said my dear.

"Well, you know," said Petia. "It's just a question."

That was the end of the conversation.

After everyone looked each other over and looked over their shoulder, after it got dark and it got light, and the road ended and the forest began, at the end of this road, in the middle of the earth, at one point, in the middle of infinity, that is, at the end of this endless road that led up to the forest and went on farther, which meant it did not end but the forest began there; infinity looked like a transformation of a thing into some other thing: where the road ended, the forest began, and where liquid ended, altitude began, and altitude could transform into time, and time could become taste, taste could become color, and there was a house there. The most incomparable view could not compare with the view that was all around. Around the house there was the view, and inside the house there was an interior, and within the interior there was a portrait. And that endless road that endlessly narrowed and led to the forest and led to the house led inside the house to the portrait, which was the dead end of this road, and in the portrait there was an endless sea, and in front of it was the portrait of a person. And the person in the portrait had his back to the sea and his face to the forest, while whoever was viewing the portrait was the other way around: he had his back to the forest and his face to the sea. And two such different views—a Middle-Russian forest and the sea—faced each other through the person looking at the portrait of the person, and the person in the portrait looking at the person.

As though out of thin air, my dear appeared, but he did not dissolve into the air, quite the opposite: the air around him seemed electrified. He was getting looks, and if he was getting them, then someone must have been sending them. Someone was. Petia was, and Yezdandukta was, and Tatya-Nyvanna was. And they were getting them too. The sisters were, and Tatya-Nyvanna was. And when Boris got the look given to Petia, then Petia did not get it the way it was intended, because Boris had his

118

own way of looking at it. And as Boris got more and more looks given to Petia by my dear, Petia was getting more and more looks from Boris. And Petia got into it, and she got involved. She did not fall in love, she did not love, but she got involved. The way you get involved in a game. And Boris was frightened to see how Petia was playing with fire, because my dear really was on fire, and Petia was melting. She blushed several times, and several times she went pale. And Petia did not notice that Boris was suffering, and Yezdandukta didn't notice it either, and even Tatya-Nyvanna didn't notice it. Because Boris was trying to conceal it to the best of his ability. He had that ability. And Petia didn't even notice how she got involved, and her sister didn't notice, because she got involved too. But everyone else noticed. Even Gleb O.R. noticed Boris's suffering, because Gleb O.R. was suffering too.

This way, with greater and greater involvement and ever greater suffering, they got to November. And in November my dear lost his head completely. He had an obsession: he had to see Petia alone and he had to tell all. Boris was not the only one suffering. The friends were all suffering, and e.s. was suffering physically because he was the only one of the friends who had had the poetry knocked out of him. When he got big—when he was a major poet—he was in such a place that after that place there was no place on his body that did not hurt; they tried to knock his soul out of him, but he put his entire soul into his poetry. They were trying to knock his poetry out along with his soul. And when he memorized his poems, they beat him and they knocked him out so that he would remember nothing of his poetry. And those who beat him were beasts, and that place was beastly. And the power was in the hands of the people who held the power in their hands. And they knocked his soul out of him along with his poetry, and they knocked his memory out of him and they mangled his life, and now he wrote poetry, but badly, but he sang well. And those who knocked the poetry out of him in the name of the authorities deserve to die. But Death isn't coming for them. Death seeks out those who deserve to live. Death looks for them and finds them, and they fall not to death but to life. Even Pushkin died of life: Death found him after life got to him. He died, and the sun of Russian poetry set. And the sun really did set, because in November days are shorter and poems are shorter, and nights are longer and dreams are longer, and everyone went off to their rooms to sleep. That left only e.s.

singing and crying, and through his tears he could see social mimicry, the disease of the Soviet people, because he could see it even better through the border, through tears. A regime that built almost nothing but destroyed almost everything—this regime of the people was hanging over the people and destroying their lives. Ration tickets for sugar soap: laughter through tears in line for life rationed out according to tickets, and he laughed if he was the last in line to laugh.

The story of Petia getting involved and becoming attracted to my dear because of his eyes, his words and, most of all, his questions and answers, was a fairly unattractive story, and fairly soon it became a simply scandalous story. Every scandal involves ladies, time, place and the weather: it was misting. My dear arranged a meeting, so it happened that Petia went to visit a certain lady but it so happened that this lady was not home, and Petia agreed to wait for her, and when, to Petia's surprise, my dear suddenly appeared in the room, he fell to his knees and embraced Petia's knees, and the things he said while standing on his knees were quite different from things he said standing up. It was a good thing that Petia managed to liberate herself from his arms, which were saying even more than his words, and that she said "No" after he said, "Yes? Yes!" Petia called for the lady of the house, but the lady of the house still wasn't there, and her daughter came instead, and Petia managed to leave all right, and when she came home, she saw that nothing at home was all right, and she decided on the spot to tell Boris everything about how nothing had happened. But she did not manage to tell him anything that day, because that day ended, and the next day also began and then ended. And the next day Boris received a letter. It was an anonymous letter. And all the friends—Gleb O.R. and False Dmitri and e.s.—got the exact same letter. The letter was a circular—that is, their entire circle of friends got this letter. The letter was composed of different words cut out of different newspapers, and its contents were flat and shocking like a newspaper's. This newspaper letter just killed Boris. It did not kill him literally, but it literally poisoned his life. The letter was hurtful. It was happy and jocular, but these sorts of jokes make you want to kill. It said that you-know-who had made a you-know-what of you-know-who. You-know-who was Petia, and you-know-what was a cuckold, and you-know-who was Boris, who was offered a membership card you-know-where, which was the cuckolds' society.

Whoever wrote this was a heartless person, meaning that he had no heart, as well as a soulless person, meaning that he had no soul. And Petia faithfully told him the truth, that she had been faithful to him. And her faithful confession only convinced Boris of what a treacherous incident this was, and the only way to end this incident was to finish off the person who had no heart. But even if you have a gun, it is difficult to aim it at the heart of a person who has no heart. Still, Boris had his heart set on a duel. His opponent really did not have a trace of heart, but suddenly his mind manifested itself, so sober and clear that it was instantly clear that the mind is bigger than the heart. My dear decided to marry none other than Petia's sister. That is, he was, of course, prepared for the duel, but he was also preparing for marriage. And it became clear to all the friends that Boris should take back his challenge since my dear had decided to marry because even though a duel is a noble undertaking, one should be mindful that a duel comes from the heart while a marriage comes from the mind. And Yezdandukta had lost her mind over my dear, and my dear was so dear to her, dressed like a London dandy,[33] he comes into the room alone, he looks around and he sees, he sees a girl that stands alone, alone she stands she stands to please, he goes up and he says cheese, and they leave the room together.

2

But there is a variety of life in life, and life manifests itself in its variety. It's as simple as that: the more there are species, orders, parties and animals, the richer life is, and the fewer there are, the less it is. And if there is only one party, one kind of sausage, one animal—a cow that lays eggs, milk and meat—then life is poorer, and being poor is a vice.

So that people would live better, so that there would be more parties, so that it would be cleaner for the animals, no matter what—what matters? All the friends in their friendly circle were awaiting a response to the letter they had sent home. This letter was friendly, written from the heart and all the emotions in it were heartfelt. While the anonymous newspaper letter was disgusting.

My dear received a response from Boris—Boris desired a duel—and my dear was not really waiting for the response to the general friendly letter to the First Person of the Year. My dear, who was not only a charming and practical-minded person but also a bit of a German, something of a foreigner, was scared of a duel more than he was scared of marriage, and it should be noted that marriage scared the hell out of him, but more than that he was scared because of a certain passage, not one that concerned the Baltics or even one that concerned the Tatars, but the one concerning the Mausoleum in Red Square. "It would be best just to bury Lenin humanely, like a human being," the friendly letter said. "Humankind has paid for his human mistakes, and there is no need to make an immortal leader out of a mortal human, and we have not paid in full." And the whole story with the anonymous letter may have seemed petty compared to the Great History that had engulfed the Motherland and even spilled over the border so that they were breaking down the wall between the Germans and the Germans, but the story with the anonymous letter had more humanity to it than does Great History, which is inhumane to humankind. In the end my dear dared to marry because he did not dare to take part in the duel, and my dear wanted to receive a different letter from Boris, one that would clearly state that Boris did not want the duel, not because my dear did not want the duel and not because my dear wanted to marry but because because why not. It is difficult to write that kind of letter, but it's not easy to receive one either. In any case, Boris and my dear did not share a table, because it would have been immoral to share a table. And when my dear got up early and had breakfast, Boris was still asleep, and when my dear left, Boris got up and had breakfast, and they did not even see each other. And though all the friends wanted them to be friends, friendship itself opposed such a friendship.

After the anonymous newspaper letter Petia was suddenly filled with the sort of affection for Boris that she had not felt before—that is, she had felt it, but that was a different kind of affection, and now this was still another kind. This was such great affection that it was big enough for more people than just Boris, and even Gleb O.R. would not have said no to this affection, and even my dear would not have said no. But Gleb O.R. summoned his strength and said no. And my dear did not summon it and did not say no. And when he continued to give Petia his old kinds of looks, Petia tried not only not to notice them herself but to make it so that others would not notice them either. The fact that Boris was her beloved and that her beloved was hurt, hurt Petia badly. Boris would leave during the day, and none of the friends knew where he went; even Petia did not know. Really, where did Boris go? Where did he go, friends?

The other friends sometimes left too, but that was clear: some were going for a walk and some were going to the store and all were going somewhere and some were going nowhere.

"My dear," e.s. said once. "You know, I'm still cutting down trees!" He said it in a sort of frightening way. He said that he had not only chopped down trees but that he had harnessed himself to the tree like a horse and dragged it and then he got porridge, and if he didn't drag it far enough he got beaten like a horse, and he showed Petia the scars on his back.

"But these are old," said Petia. "Those beatings were a long time ago."

"My dear," said e.s. "What does a long time mean?"

Really, what does "a long time" mean in terms of infinity, if this "long time" is less than a second or even less than that. And even if a person dragging logs has not dragged them for forty years and has not been beaten for forty years, then in infinity he is beaten more and more, or he is fed porridge every second.[34]

"What kind of porridge?"

"Porridge-schmoriidge."

"Would you sing something?" asked Petia.

"Well, what shall I sing for you, my dear?"

"Sing something you like."

And the fact is that if an airplane has flown once, it is forever flying, and that if a bird has sung once, it is forever singing, and that if one has killed oneself once, one is killing forever, and that if one has died once, one is dead forever, and that if one has lived once, one is alive forever, and so on, and infinity stretches far, etc. etc. And if Petia was still the same Petia who loved Boris, and if Boris was still the same poor Boris except that he was rich, then Yezdandukta was not at all the same old Yezdandukta who had loved Boris; she was an entirely different Yezdandukta, who had found someone entirely different to be to her liking. And there was never any need for Yezdandukta to love Boris wholeheart-edly as a person: she should have just found a different person and loved him as a person. Because Petia did not love Boris as a person; she loved him as Boris. Because there was no other person on Earth who could be Boris, as well as no other Boris who could be this kind of person. Her feelings for him welled up in her chest in such a way that they could cause tears to well up in her eyes. And when among all these living people some living people suddenly died, becoming dead, one could grow scared for the living people among all these dead people, because there were a lot fewer living people among dead people than dead people among living people. And though the number of living people was growing, the number of dead people was also growing... And the proportion of the number of living people to the number of dead people was proportional. So if you imagine a fraction where the numerator (the one on top, as in fact they are on top—on the ground) is the number of living people and the denominator (the one on the bottom, as they really are on the bottom—underground) is the number of dead people, then the number that you get when you divide the number of living people by the number of dead people will in all likelihood be irrational, and the remainder will probably extend to infinity, and for every dead person there will always be zero-point—an infinite number of figures after the decimal point of the living.

There was beauty in art, and there used to be beauty in architecture too, and generally, the forests used to be dark and the cathedrals used to be beautiful, and now all the most pathetic and colorless things are beauty, all the ugliness is beauty. And if you find a piece of rusted metal and bring it home and hang it up, that will be beautiful too; the main thing is to find the right thing and hang it right... And it was not just Lenin in the Mausoleum that the friendly letter addressed; it also addressed the Mausoleum itself, the one where Lenin lies, and it said that so many lies have been told from the balcony of the Mausoleum that even if from now on every word issuing from that balcony were to be true, it would be difficult to believe these truths, and that it would truly be better if truth issued not from the balcony but from some place else; granted, there has to be an elevated surface from which truth issues, there has to be a sort of hilly thing, and the Mausoleum had been this mount. But it would still be better if that hill were razed. Nothing blasphemous would be necessary, no explosions to remember it by,[35] but the Mausoleum should just be moved to a cemetery, where it belongs along with all the lies issued from the balcony, which should also be buried in the cemetery. That's all. They said their piece. Except that was not all. It would also be a good thing if the First Person of the

Year became the first person to turn down having a grave by the Kremlin, because it is unbecoming to be laid to rest near the Kremlin, and consequently it is unethical and even unsanitary to be laid to rest near the Kremlin, as well as uncompassionate and unkind to be there until the end of time.

In a kind of dining room some people who were kind of friends were eating some kind of meat and drinking wine of the port kind, seated around a round table. This was a one-of-a-kind situation, kind of unlike ones that had taken place earlier, kind of like the kind that had not yet taken place.

But Boris was not home yet. It was already night. At night everything grew quieter, and people spoke less and were silent more, and it happened more that one person would be talking while everyone else was silent, while in the mornings it was the opposite: one person would be silent while everyone else was talking, and in the mornings things got louder more often.

This house is in the middle of a garden, this garden is in the middle of a country, this country is in the middle of the Earth, which has no boundaries. There is so much sun and water here. And so much earth. The earth here is in the middle of sun and water. It is winter again. And if winter is when emotions quiet down, and if spring is when they wake up, then winter is when they are shut down. They sleep. That's what winter is about. That's what snow is for.

The friends were just like other people in that they loved it when the sun was bright and the sea was warm and the wind was light, and the friends were just like other people in that they did not like it when the wind was blasting and the sun was cold and the sea was frightful. And Boris never did appear, not even on the horizon or in the future or in nature—it seemed he did not exist in nature, and this didn't seem like him. Nature was sleeping. The friends whiled away long evenings doing everything and nothing. My dear, who did nothing, wandered around the building looking at everything other people were doing: e.s. did a bit of singing, Petia did a bit of drawing, Gleb O.R. wrote something—perhaps poetry, perhaps not—and Tatya-Nyvanna also started doing a bit of drawing, though drawing was not really what she was into. She was into coloring inside the lines. She colored in boxes, and she put dots in some of them but not in others. Yezdandukta was really not into this kind of life: she was visibly aging while Tatya-Nyvanna was visibly getting prettier. And

125

the aged Yezdandukta and the beautified Tatya-Nyvanna would sometimes exchange a few words. Women's issues, which interested both of them, did not interest the other friends much. And the friends rarely listened to their talks—though mostly Yezdandukta did the talking while Tatya-Nyvanna mostly did the being quiet. But the friends were not listening to what Yezdandukta was talking about and what Tatya-Nyvanna was quiet about. With the exception of those times when Yezdandukta talked loudly and Tatya-Nyvanna was loudly quiet. And the fact that women needed their freedom to be equal with men and that men should also be equal with men and that no, women don't want to become men, they just want to become people, while men just want to be men and only then to be people. And for that reason a woman's journey was shorter than a man's. Bon voyage!

And Tatya-Nyvanna rarely argued, and Yezdandukta sometimes even had arguments with herself. She would argue a bit and then she would be convinced, or else she wouldn't. And what was False Dmitri doing now? Which Dmitri was he passing himself off as? As a different one, not even the same one as before, but the later one.

And the later Boris came back, the later everyone went to bed. As soon as he came, everyone went to bed. Only my dear went to bed earlier. He always went to bed earlier than Boris came home later.

And time dragged on, as did the evenings, as did thoughts. And Boris was dragging his feet on responding, and my dear was dragging his feet on getting married. And all of this could have dragged on and on, if Boris had not suddenly up and responded to the disgusting newspaper letter. And his response was exactly what my dear expected. His response was horrifyingly noble, awfully honest and terribly beautiful. In his response Boris wrote clearly that he was withdrawing his challenge because he did not consider the letter to be insulting to him. He was hit on one cheek and he turned the other. He turned the other cheek for the other blow. The wedding was a blow to Boris. The wedding was supposed to help everyone make peace. It was supposed to be as though my dear had just suddenly fallen in love with Yezdandukta—no, it was supposed to be as though he loved Petia and as though Petia loved him too, and as though Boris didn't notice this, so Petia and my dear could see each other as though nothing had happened, as though there had been no disgustingly anonymous letter, as though everything were fine and as though all the friends were happy that everything had turned out so well and as though Boris were no longer coming home late and my dear did not have to go to bed early so they could greet each other as though they were friends. But all of this was just how it was supposed to be.

And it was as though all of this were happening not here, abroad, but there, at home, as though this mess with the wedding were added to the whole mess at home; and it was frightening to look at the people crammed into the Metro and think of war, as though the war had begun in the Metro, as though the dead bodies piled on top of one another at rush hour could not even make a sound, as though this perverted regime had perverted the natural ways of life, as though perversions were being perverted and gays were becoming lesbians and lesbians were becoming gays, and as though the salaries paid to Soviet people were not salaries but compensation for the fact that Soviet life was bad for people, and as though it was bad for people to live off this compensation, and as though there were ever more bad people and ever fewer bad animals. As though all this were for real.

But really it was all really nice. Charming. Glorious. Amazing.

And just wonderful. All right. Bearable.

After Boris sent the letter withdrawing his challenge, my dear felt victorious and Boris felt defeated. And Petia loved Boris. At this moment, during the storm, when passions were running high—to duel or not to duel; to be or not to be—Petia embraced him and he came back; that was precisely the sequence of events: first she embraced him and then he came back, not that first he came back and then she embraced him.

But there was one thing. The house started falling apart. Whereas before it had been divided into the male and female halves, now everything collapsed and got all mixed up. The half of the house that was female became half-male, and the half of the house that was male lost more than half of the male half of the population. Everything was mixed up: False Dmitri was reunited with Tatya-Nyvanna, my dear and Yezdandukta found their place under the sun, and Gleb O.R. had no attachment at all to any particular place: his place was his workplace, where he could either write or read: either or. And e.s. suited his place in the manner of a person who suits his place more than his place

127

suits him. Petia and Boris were the only ones who could not find their place in either half, so they kept going from place to place.

And when Petia embraced Boris when he returned, when the sun was flat up in the sky and one could only guess (if one knew) at the fact that it had volume, for some reason the stars and the sky, which did not seemed flat—it seemed right away like it was a sort of convex concave, and it probably was not the sky at all but the street that smelled like narcissus and melted snow, and this smell permeated the home—but not the common European home, which is only a plan that will stand forever once it is built, but the house that had just about collapsed but was still barely standing—a private house. It was an incredible smell: it smelled like spring in Moscow when Petia loved Boris and the snow was black with dirt and the smell of narcissus mixed with exhaust, and women, who were not yet extinct and were more like cats while men were more like dogs, and if both are species, if woman is of the cat species while the dog is a Negro, an Indian, a European and a husband, just let the last of the cat species and the dog species and the other species become extinct...

Petia and Boris seceded, receded and succeeded, and they had a turkey in the oven, and this turkey was a sculpture—no, it was a structure consisting of a solid construction—bones—and of soft meat, and it was heating and melting and dripping metal fat, and it was edible. And if a rabbit can fly, it has edible wings; and if a chicken stands on all fours, it has edible extra legs; and a piglet stuffed with lamb that can swim like a fish, and all food stuffs that swim, fly and chirp—they do it all to be eaten, drunk and washed down, bon appetit!

The bird that would never fly again was hissing in the oven; the friends had all flitted off. The house was deserted. Whose house was it. Who knew. And who knew whose world this was? Snow was flying outside the window. It was flying off and new snow was flying in. The snow had wings, and it was using them to fly. And even if this world is blown to pieces and people's arms and legs fly off, the snow will continue to fly in every winter and fly away every spring. And last year's snow, like last year's thinking, like yesterday's news reminded one of the days of yesteryear.

"You are always going somewhere," Petia said to Boris. "Where?"

"Yeah, somewhere."

"But where, I don't know, where?"

"Where do I go?"

"Yes, you go somewhere every day, and you are not here."

"I work."

"Where you go—you work there?"

"Every day."

"It's far away somewhere. It's late."

"It's not so far."

"Is there a house there?"

"Maybe there is a house."

"Do you work in that house?"

"Not just in the house."

"Outside the house too?"

"Inside and outside."

"Let's go there."

"Where?"

"Where you go."

"You want to walk?"

"Do we have to walk there?"

"I don't know where you want to go."

"I want to go where you go where nobody knows where it is."

"No, it's too far to walk, and it's late."

"You have to ride in something?"

"You can get a ride and then walk."

"Where?"

"We can walk somewhere."

"Let's go."

And while the uneaten bird cooled off, going cold turkey off hot lamb, Petia and Boris left the house and marched off into the distance.

The light was lightly rocking the illuminated road and the buildings along it. The light penetrated to the very heart of the road. Petia and Boris walked, and the road led them. It led them far away from the house, to another road, which led to other buildings, a whole bed of buildings—these were tall white buildings, very fragile ones, and not just because of the light falling on these buildings, and not just because of the snow flying over these buildings; below these buildings there were trees, which surrounded the buildings like shrubbery, and there was one building that stood at the highest point in this garden of buildings.

"See?" said Boris. "That's the building."

129

Unlike the other buildings, the windows in this building were not illuminated, with the exception of one window, located around the fifth-floor level—it had a light deep inside, a small light—a night light or a desk lamp—and this light lit up the whole building.

This window was like Petia's window in Moscow, in her building, except it was as though this building were uninhabited, as though it stood as a monument to a past life.

"I see," said Petia.

Perhaps it was the light, but this building was like the fog, except this fog had a firm shape, which kept the building from fading.

"It looks like your building."

"From a distance," said Petia, "it does."

This garden of buildings with the single building at the top of the garden was circled by a river, which looked decorative too, with its little paper boats chased down the river by the wind. And someone had sent out paper airplanes, which were flying over the river. But who? Who set the boats to float? And to get to the building garden one had to cross over a bridge that someone had constructed over the river, and there was a moon hanging over that bridge. But who hung that moon? The moon crossed the river and started rising over the building garden, and when it stopped over the very top, over the building, which stood at the very top, it stayed there a bit and then it started descending on the other side of the garden and disappeared into where a forest flowed. Rivers grow and forests flow. The flow of time. As it flowed on, Petia and Boris turned back, and all that was left of the turkey were the wings, because the friends had come home earlier and eaten supper, leaving them wings for their supper, but the wings could not satisfy their hunger—they could only satisfy their thirst, so they drank the wings and ate some wine left over from the friends. And after they had a bite to eat and a bit to drink, they saw a strip of light coming into the room from the other room, and in that strip of light stood an android, stripped of volume, cutting the darkness with light like the strip and transmitting sound with his very being, like an antenna. Waves of light and waves of sound were emanating from him.

"Andy-baby," Petia called out to him. "Here, kitty-kitty-kitty."

But there are things in this world of dreams that you can't joke with because they are no joke. They can bite. And the andy-baby can bite, using light and sound. For him people are mere objects within his field, and people are not supposed to joke with him because he can play jokes on people himself. And the field, which is stormy like the sea, with sea waves out in the field, and the sea, which flowers like a field—these too are not to be joked with. We are supposed to live seriously and die as a joke—a nasty joke.

Petia and Boris retired to their room, which they had been calling theirs for a time, since the time when my dear started calling Yezdandukta his. A room of one's own always has its own charm.

Boris looked at his paintings, and Petia looked at hers, and it was not yet all that light, and the paintings looked like engravings, which have only light and dark areas, light and shadow, but no color. And Petia and Boris were not in color either—they were black-and-white, light-and-dark, though Petia was lighter and Boris was darker, and when they pulled the blanket over themselves, they both became dark in the dark, though now, in the dark, Boris, on top, was lighter than Petia, who was, on the bottom, darker than the Borovitsky Hill,[36] which was, at the top of Moscow, lighter than Moscow itself, which could be viewed from the top of it, and the hill, which was settling by so many millimeters a year, was moving and not standing still, because all the excess weight on top of it was pushing down on it with all its weight, and this weight was driving it underground—the excess weight of the Mausoleum and the excess weight of the Palace of Congresses, and the excess weight of the tanks and machine guns that trudged from right to left (if you faced the Savior Gate tower) every year—and if it were not for this excess weight, the hill would not be settling so fast, because beauty is not heavy—St. Basil's Cathedral is not heavy, and the Kremlin is not—and you could walk up the hill lightly, and lightly walk through the Savior Gate, taking off your hat, which even the tsar himself used to take off—to become even lighter—but not in light of the black wagons that press down on the hill with their tires and drive through the gate without taking off their hats. People on one side and wheels on the other; one entrance for wheels and another exit for people. Enter on the other side. Go around. Detour. No entry. Enter around the corner. No bags allowed. Closed for renovations. Spring cleaning. And the noise over the blanket was not just any noise but the noise made by the andy-baby taking a walk on the surface of the blanket. He strolled among the waves of the blan-

131

ket; he liked to play jokes on his objects, so he trudged like a tank—from right to left—and his weight made the hill under the blanket settle. It was dark under the blanket, and who knows how many dimensions there are in the dark: points and lines? lines and areas? areas and volumes? and when it became hard to breathe under the blanket, Boris started constructing a model in the air, a model of little cubes that formed a cube that could be seen from all angles at one time. At the same time, the cube was not transparent. If you enlarged the blanket surface and viewed it from above, like from an airplane, it would be quite picturesque. A stray silver coin glistened like a lake surrounded by loose tobacco in the image of a sandy rim, and beyond the lake a matchbox stuck out, lonely like a building. And when this landscape began to grow and settle on the ground like a real landscape lit by a real sun up in the real sky, Petia and Boris hugged each other good-bye before going to sleep, because who knows what awaits us in sleep and afterward, and when they really fell asleep, they became sleeping people, and who knows who those people are when they are asleep.

And in the dark of sleep the friendly letter seemed perfectly innocent in their sleep, and if in their sleep the black, the white and the yellow slaughtered each other, and in sleep all the people and all the other people were pagans, including thieves, polygamists, slaves, prostitutes, pirates, then the one request voiced in their sleep could have seemed utterly impossible, but what if they were awake? This one request the friends voiced in their friendly letter seemed impossible even if they were awake. All the other requests could be fulfilled, but if this request were to be fulfilled, they would need to be transformed instantly, in their sleep, from pagans into Christians. The friendly letter on the issue of repealing the death penalty said that, contrary to what some people may think, this would be good not for them but for us. Because there is them and there is us, and they are the ones who kill, and it's us who might be killed. And if they knew that, no matter what, we would not kill them no matter what they did, they would not do what they would have done if they had known that we would kill them anyway. And if they knew that never in their lives, not in their earthly lives nor in their eternal life, not on their lives, will they ever be killed, that neither in this life nor in their eternal life will they ever pay for their sin and that their sin will continue to weigh on their hearts up in heaven and down under ground, and if they knew that they will never be able to pay for their sin even if the price were their own lives— that would be the most frightful of punishments, because those who are killed are alive anyway and those who kill are dead.

The tram goes back and forth, and these people go this way and those people go that way, and these people could not be those people so they would not have to go from here to there, those people could not be these people and not go from there to here. Same thing.

And while Petia and Boris slept in each other's arms, the sun came up, and the eternal issue of sex in the night air, where there are night lights and women and men and lovers, was replaced by a non-issue in the light of day, which illuminates mommies and daddies and schoolboys and schoolgirls.

And it was not until the morning of the night that was the following night that Petia and Boris were awakened by love. This was the real thing, which began with desire and continued and ended with declarations of love, and for some reason it refused to end, this love would not be satisfied, even when it flitted off and their bodies cooled, it rushed back in and it all started over from the beginning, like at the very beginning of love. Petia begged this love for Boris, and Boris begged it for Petia. And this love gave them to each other. And at the moment of love they did everything love ordered them to do to each other, and they carried out all its orders with love, and even when Petia did not want to do something but love wanted it, Petia did it, and Boris did everything love demanded, and love was very demanding. And the moment it demanded it, Boris ended up at the end of Petia and she ended up at the beginning of Boris, and then Petia was at the end of Boris and he was at the beginning of Petia. Love turned them every which way, and they let it play with them, but this was not a playful game but a very serious one, which they played seriously and with abandon, and they called it by name and it loved them, thank you, thank them. And when they tired of it and it abandoned them, it returned immediately. And even when love had already taken place, they wanted it as though it had not, and it drove them to total declarations of love, and now they had nothing to hide from it, not the fact that they belonged to it, that they were willing to give themselves over to it over and over, and it was not lying when it said that it loved them, they knew this for a fact even when they let it violate them and when they let it not violate them. They were three. It used them as it pleased, and they surrendered to its desires because these were their desires. All the words Boris said to Petia were the words of love, and all the words Petia said to him were its words. The three of them were material. And it pushed Petia and Boris so close together that not even a finger could fit between them—there was no empty space between them except for the happy emptiness in their eyes. But eyes are not space—but what are they?

And then love went so far that it confused them and Petia no longer knew where Boris ended and Petia began. They began together and they ended together, and when it called for Petia, Boris answered—he said, "That's me," but me does not have a gender, either masculine or feminine, me is just me, the genesis of any gender, and Boris could be any Petia, and Petia could be any Boris, and they were driven to this by love, and by the time they got there, they had used so many words, though these were the same words over and over again, and because there were few of them—"I love you"—they had to be said many times, but the word love repeated a hundred times did not satisfy love, because it loved them and demanded a repeat performance. Why did it choose them? did they suit its taste in people or was it the way they tasted? And love left a taste in their mouths that was the taste of love, an incomparable taste. And the fact is there are paintings that use little paint, and there is music that uses few notes, and there is love that uses few words, because there are only three of them. And what it did to them then was something truly incredible: it took their innocence in those places that were still innocent. It turned out Petia had a place like that. And so did Boris. There they were before it, no longer innocent in any way, but neither were they guilty, because this was love, which is entitled to anything during love. And even when, upon awakening, it abandoned them, in reality it did not abandon them but took them to a dreamy place where, in their dreams, it continued to perform miracles of love, because it was a southern night on the train and their compartment had no roof over their heads: above them stars floated slowly by, and the train was pushing its way through a thicket—that is, there were tree branches with dark leaves right over their heads, and these branches were getting inside the compartment through the roof, and they were rustling, and the train rustled going through this forest, but this rustle was soft, as though the train were just passing by instead of rushing

134

through, as though it were walking. There was only one couchette in the compartment, and it was not all that narrow, so that if they embraced they had enough room, and Petia and Boris made themselves comfortable on this couchette and kissed against the wind that blew in through the missing roof, and this little wind bothered them so that they glomped onto each other in this motion, in this rocking. They rocked in tune with the train, and the depth of it all made their hearts beat faster and faster, and then there was this one position of Petia's in which she ended up on the bottom lying on her stomach facing the door and Boris was on top also facing the door and then it turned out that the door was missing and that in its place there was a light curtain that was blowing in the wind, and Petia and Boris were in a position in which other passengers could see them, and Petia felt ashamed and Boris was utterly without shame, so he refused to let her go but covered her with his body and continued to do as he would have if there had been no passengers passing by the door, and he grabbed her hand and all of Boris was concentrated in Petia's hand, which started doing its thing without any regard for Petia, who could no longer hear what Boris was whispering and the fact of the passengers passing by the door and witnessing the facts occurring when the curtain blew away—it mattered. No matter what, the things all over the floor were rolling all over the floor, and on one foot Petia had a boot that was pressed up against the pillow, and her other foot was hanging off the couchette, because the couchette beneath them started narrowing drastically and narrowed to the point that now only one person could possibly fit on it, and now Petia and Boris were forced to lie on top of each other all the time, and when Boris's foot pressed up against Petia's boot, it became clear that Boris and Petia themselves were not made of wood. They tried to keep from moving to avoid being noticed by the passengers who were strolling, smoking and talking in the corridor— what were they talking about? They were talking in a foreign language. They were an audience. Not human at all. They were so foreign that Petia and Boris could love each other in front of them without shame. And Petia and Boris were certainly not intended for the foreigners, but the foreigners were certainly intended for Petia and Boris. And this lascivious idea meant that they could be as loud as they wanted, but they wanted to keep being quiet. And everything that was barely moving and everything that was hardly moving at all, and everything that was falling off and put on and taken off and everything that was under, over and in was required for the work they were doing, which was their lives' work, and this was their life. And after they were finished, the curtain turned wooden and turned into a door, and the foreigners went back to their foreign lands, the roof closed over the compartment, the trees took their places along the railroad tracks, dreams took their places alongside awakening and a new day began.

3

After this kind of love, when Petia and Boris got it all together and went to sleep together, for some reason they woke up separately.

"I wonder if Pushkin smoked."

"He drank and played cards. He probably smoked too."

"So you think he smoked?"

"Never thought about it," said Boris and started thinking: Did Pushkin smoke or not? Boris was still asleep and as he put Petia to sleep with his sleeping, he slept a bit more: If Pushkin had smoked, then Eugene Onegin would have smoked as well as Boris Godunov and the Bronze Horseman, though the Bronze Horseman did in fact smoke while Natalya Nikolayevna did not smoke and Masha Mironova didn't and Tanya and Petrusha didn't, while Shvabrin[37] did, and he was bad, and smoking is bad.

Boris was lying separately from Petia, on the edge of the bed, and even his arms and legs lay separately. And Petia was lying separately from his arms and legs, against the wall. Boris got up first, while Petia got up second, and Boris washed up and shaved while Petia brushed her hair. And Boris was the first to get dressed. And they each had their own clothes, and their clothes could not have mistaken them for each other, and they could not have mistaken their clothes. And Boris was the first to say, "I'm going to go now." And Petia did not say anything. And Boris started getting ready to go—he was packing his bag and he got readier and readier—and Petia watched him getting ready to go. And when he was finally ready, Petia turned around to see how sad it was out the window so that Boris could not see how sad she was. And suddenly Boris said, "Get ready." She was so happy she

136

was ready in a split second. And even things that had never zipped up quickly zipped up in a split second. She was ready right then and there. "Where are we going?" asked Petia when they had already walked away from the house. They walked and walked and Boris was not telling where they were going, though he of course knew where they were going, while Petia did not and simply went wherever he led her. He led her to a building that was an ordinary nine-story tower, a white matchbox of a building. They went inside and what they saw inside was what Petia had only heard about before: the Kolomensky Temple in a box. They stood inside the box, inside the temple, and Petia pointed out one unfinished dome. Tiny people were crawling on the walls and slapping the walls with their tiny trowels—that is, the people just seemed tiny because they were high up. Petia and Boris stood at the bottom while people crawled around at the top, and from the top they could see how small Petia and Boris were at the bottom. But they were all, every single one of them, real. And the temple was real: it was really built. The walls were white like the air and the blue dome was blue like the sky and it had stars of gold like the stars. And at this moment in the temple Petia started loving Boris even more than she had loved him in bed, because now her soul was singing, while in bed her body had sung. And her soul now wanted to sing something to her body. And everyone was now busy building what Boris alone had thought up: a hundred people were building something that a single person had made up, and it was for all the people together. And the fact that Boris had not wanted to show Petia something that wasn't finished was even better than the fact that he now showed it to her. It was a process in the process of life in the process of work in the process of love. And Petia kissed Boris the way she had kissed him a long long time ago that time in his studio when they were in the box, in the model of the temple, except then the temple wasn't real, though back then and now they always kissed for real. The coat was all covered with whitewash because if you lean against the wall whitewash gets on your clothes and that's exactly what they were doing—leaning against the wall because this was the best way to kiss. And the people who were working might have seen that they were kissing, but they were working, so they did not see. And Petia and Boris were kissing and did not see that the people were working. But they were doing good work. And Petia and Boris were having a good kiss.

When e.s. woke up, the essential supply of life awoke in him, and he launched into a song. The fact that he had been beaten in his life, that he had not been beaten in thirty years; what is thirty years against eternity? he had been beaten for life, for thirty years ahead thirty years ago. No one had the sort of love that could make him feel loved enough so he would no longer feel beaten, and even his own poems were not lovely enough; they made him forget about living so he would forget how to write poetry. Now he was just like an ordinary person who did not know how to write poetry. They took the poet out of him as though the poet had been sitting inside him and they had knocked him around until they knocked the poet out of him, and they knocked the person around too, but the person survived, because people are better suited to living than poets, even though poets are more alive than people. It would not be right to say that e.s. was a dead person, because in fact he was a real person—he was just a dead poet, and he was not alien to anything human, but he was alien to everything poetic. e.s. sat there and imbibed, gulping down glass after glass, and as a person he didn't give a damn about anything. Little by little he was becoming extinct, both as a person and as the person who is the crown of creation. This was a weakness. But this was his own personal weakness; it was not the common weakness of all people. If all people at once developed a weakness for such weakness and they all stopped giving a damn, that would be when they became extinct—a few specimens would remain, of course, but nothing human would be left of humankind except for skulls and bones.

And when Petia and Boris came back home, the friends thought about what to do until they thought of something to do. They thought they would have a friendly outing where all the friends together would go out into the world. The world was on the side—that side of society that has coming-out parties, not on the side of home but on the other side of the tracks. Nighttime came and brought nighttime activities, and all the friends decided to go out on the occasion of—well, there is always an occasion. It was a suitable occasion: my dear and Yezdandukta were engaged. Petia decided to come along because she could not say no to her sister, and Boris could not say no to Petia, so all together they decided in favor of the outing. And False Dmitri and

Tatya-Nyvanna were just a wonderful couple, the kind that's welcome anywhere anytime.

And Gleb O.R. decided that since everything was already decided, he was not so decisive as to stay home alone. So it was decided. And it was raining. And it was snowing. And the wind was blowing, and the rain was falling and so was everything else.

"Aren't you happy?" Petia asked Boris.

There really was no happiness in him. He was going along with everyone so he would not fall behind, because everyone was going together.

"But we are together," said Petia.

"Together with everyone else," said Boris.

"With you."

"Of course I'm happy," said Boris. "Of course I am."

How could one not be happy that everything had come to such a happy ending? And my dear and Yezdandukta found each other in the end and were now in peace and left everyone else in peace too. But there was no peace in Boris's soul. His soul knew something but did not know how to tell Petia's soul, which knew nothing of it. The party was held in a beautiful house, and there were beautiful dishes on the table, and there were beautiful dresses on the young girls, and the ladies were polite and the men were gallant, and the men were drinking out of the goblets, which were bigger, and the ladies were drinking out of the tumblers, which were smaller. And e.s. was supposed to sing and the guests were supposed to dance, because that's what e.s. was invited for and that's what the guests were invited for, but who were the hosts that had invited everyone for a reason? And my dear was darling. He acted like a fiancé and a lover, and like a future husband and a future lover. Except that he acted like a fiancé and a future husband in relation to Yezdandukta and like a lover and a future lover in relation to Petia. He had not forgotten about his affair with Petia; on the contrary, at the party he acted like it was a current affair. But Petia was having a great time and did not understand why Boris was grim, and when he asked, "What do you want?" and Petia said, "I want women, wine, coffee and cigarettes," Boris was not happy to hear this joke and Petia said, "That's a joke," but it was no joke to Boris while it was a joke to Petia, so she kept joking around, and life seemed like a joke and the joke seemed to be life.

And when e.s. suddenly broke into tears in the middle of a

139

song, even though it was a joke song, he himself started cracking jokes about his tears. He joked and cried, and cried and sang, and sang and joked. He was crying because life was no joke, and he was singing because the joke was not a song. The party was a success! And when all the happy guests proceeded to the small hall where beer was served, my dear joked that beer was best drunk in the john among toilets so that the beer could flow in and flow out at the same time in the same place, and that if beer was drunk on the beach then it was necessary to swim all the time, and that if beer was drunk in a meadow then it was necessary to go in the shade, and to go in the meadow if it was drunk in the shade. And his joke did not sound dirty, because he himself was pure and beautiful and a genius—he was the genius of pure beauty. While my dear danced with Petia, Gleb O.R., Boris—Gleb or Boris—smoked and Yezdandukta sang with e.s. and Tatya-Nyvanna and False Dmitri ate and drank, and everyone had had so much to drink and to eat and to dance and to kiss that it was time to go home but my dear married Yezdandukta that evening on the spot and that same evening on that same spot proposed to Petia that she should belong to him that same evening—and this was purely a joke, and Boris thought that all of it together was dirty. And if my dear was to maintain his purity after his joke, he had to be killed, pure and simple, killing his purely joking joke along with him, which was what Boris was on his way to doing that evening, purely so that my dear and all his dirty ways would be gone from this pure world.

But the world was dirty. And no one will ever know the truth about their duel. Because that same evening, at dawn, after the party, Boris and my dear went off to their duel, but something kept coming between the opponents, and this something was the andy-baby, and when Boris started to aim, the andy-baby turned so that he turned into a plane and my dear ended up shielded by the andy-baby, and when, on the other hand, my dear took aim, the andy-baby turned so that Boris was, at gun point, completely open, because at that moment this android was a line in relation to Boris. And the andy-baby kept turning this way and that, and one moment he shielded Boris with his plane and my dear was open, and the next moment, it was Boris who was open and my dear who was shielded, because the two-dimensional andy-baby, who consisted of a line and a plane, kept setting up both opponents as luck would have it, and luck was in the andy-baby himself, and the andy-baby was in luck. And my dear could pay for his sins only with his death, and Boris could avenge himself only with his life. But everything happened the other way around. Boris fired a shot and missed, while my dear fired a shot and did not miss. And he did not hit the andy-baby; he hit Boris, and Boris fell. He fell, but he did not die right away. And when they brought him home, Petia could feel that he was dying. He had an open wound in his stomach, and at this moment all of him was open to her, and she saw in this open wound that there was a bad connection in his stomach so that some of the time there was a spark and some of the time it wasn't there, and there was power in his stomach, and some of the time it was there and some of the time it disappeared, and as long as there was a spark and there was a connection, Boris was alive, but suddenly the spark started appearing less and less: something inside him disconnected, and the power disappeared, but where did it go? really, where?

Petia cried and cried. Oh, how she cried. Only Boris could have consoled her, but he was already dead, and now there was no one to console her. She cried inconsolably. She would start to cry, and when she was already stopping, she would start to cry again. The way she cried was not the way e.s. cried, because he sang softly and cried quietly, while she did not sing; she just cried and cried. Whatever she did, she cried as she did it, and she had many things to do, and sometimes she cried like a person with a lot to do: she did something fast and cried fast. That is, she cried all the time. Of course it was the worst for Boris, who could not be with Petia because he was dead, but it was the worst for Petia, who could not be with Boris because she was alive.

And the friends in their entire circle of friends suddenly remembered about the friendly letter they had sent home, and they couldn't help crying when they thought of it. Because the letter was no joke. And the friends could also have cried if their letter had been treated as a joke. Or as a nasty joke. And Boris was killed because life had seemed like a joke. And there were not enough tears to cry about this joke. Because life was certainly no joke and the tears that cried for this life were a joke compared to life.

And the sound of the train that sounded like the sea making sounds with the rocking of the wheels, and the rocking of the sea rocking like the train with the splashing of waves—all this was the same, but there was no Boris. Petia distanced herself from Boris

141

in rhythm with the beating of her heart—but this was literature. Poor Boris—he was poor not because he died rich, but because he died. And then came the eclipse of the moon, which occurs along with the darkening of the heart more often than with the eclipse of the mind. The darkening of the moon. And the heart, which was still light, shone like a full moon rid of the shadow of another heart. The shadow crept off the heart that had darkened another heart. And the shadow of Boris that had been on Petia's heart crept off with the noise of the receding train, which receded into the distance but was not real because in reality it was carrying neither Petia nor Boris, because in reality, even if Petia was somewhere, there was no Boris anywhere. And along with the first rays, with the sun, black-and-white people went out into the street; these were two races—black and white—but both the blacks and the whites had the same gray shadows, and the shadows of the blacks were no blacker, and the shadows of the whites were no whiter.

And when he died and they brought him there for the viewing, it looked like he was finished, like everything in him that was unfinished was just the way it should be, that nothing should be changed because if anything was done just to make it better it would only make it worse. And his burial service was held in his temple, the one he had built, the one that was a temple on the inside and an ordinary matchbox of a building on the outside, where it looked like stone, and Boris himself at that moment was Boris only on the inside, while on the outside he, too, was an ordinary box of a person who looked like stone.

And the birds were singing. And the people came and started singing as well. And it sounded good. Even those who couldn't sing sounded good. And when the people finished singing and the birds finished singing and flew away, the people flew away as well.

NOTES

1. The protagonist of Dostoevsky's *Crime and Punishment*, who at the beginning of the novel murders an old woman and her sister.

2. A group of Russian officers who led a military uprising against the Tsar in 1825 in St. Petersburg's Senate Square.

3. All Russian schoolchildren memorize a quote from Ivan Turgenev, in which he defines the Russian language as "great and mighty."

4. The Gold Star, given to a Hero of the Soviet Union or Hero of Socialist Labor, was the highest military or civilian honor in the Soviet Union. The Ushakov Medal and St. George Cross were tsarist medals of honor.

5. Boris and Gleb are Russian Orthodox saints.

6. Nineteenth-century writer and philosopher Alexander Herzen. Lenin wrote of Herzen that he had been "awakened" by the Decembrists. A 1970s satirical poem by the émigré poet Naum Korzhavin creates an entire chain of "awakenings," beginning with the Decembrists and ending with Lenin himself, and concludes that "No one in Russia should ever be awakened."

7. The restaurant's name means "Anchor."

8. The term *homo sovietikus* was introduced by Alexander Zinovyev, a dissident and then an émigré writer, to define what he believed was a unique type of human animal created by the Soviet state.

9. Stalin's reign of terror is known in Russia as the Cult of Personality—a term coined by Nikita Khrushchev.

10. The writer is Vladimir Nabokov, and the book is his novel, *Glory*.

11. The American publishing house Ardis published books in Russian as well as in English in the 1970s and 1980s, including those by Nabokov.

12. Russian Orthodox Easter sometimes falls on May 1, International Workers Solidarity Day, a state holiday in the Soviet Union.

13. Countess Mary is a character from *A Hero of Our Time*, a novel by Mikhail Lermontov; Anna Karenina is the protagonist of *Anna Karenina*, a novel by Lev Tolstoy.

14. Alexander Pushkin was the great-great-grandson of an Abyssinian man brought to Russia during Peter the Great's reign.

15. A line from a Pushkin poem.

16. Pushkin was killed in a duel with a convoluted prehistory. In November 1936 Pushkin received three copies of an anonymous letter stating he had become a member of the cuckolds' society. The poet concluded that the letter was a reference to the persistent attentions his wife had been receiving from Baron Georges D'Anthès, the adopted son of the Dutch ambassador to Russia. Pushkin banned D'Anthès from his house but later, because the gossip persisted, challenged D'Anthès to a duel. D'Anthès accepted. Soon, however, he became engaged to Pushkin's sister-in-law, and, upon learning of this engagement, the poet withdrew his challenge. Relations did not improve, however; the rumors regarding Pushkin's wife's behavior did not cease, and two weeks after D'Anthès's wedding, Pushkin wrote an insulting letter to the Dutch ambassador, whom he perceived as scheming against him. In response, D'Anthès challenged Pushkin to a duel, which took place on January 27, 1837.

17. Selective highlights from Vladimir Lenin's biography.

18. Throughout the 1820s Pushkin encountered problems with the authori-

ties, having his verse censored and even being exiled to southern Russia as punishment for politically indiscreet pronouncements. Official Soviet literary criticism made much of this, all but claiming that Pushkin was indeed killed by the tsar's regime rather than D'Anthès's bullet.

19. A reference to the Russian text of the Communist anthem, the *Internationale*, which contains the line: "He who is nothing will become everything."

20. Among the many passages in the body of Russian literature devoted to the killing of Pushkin, this one, from Marina Tsvetaeva's essay "My Pushkin," is probably most helpful at sketching in some of the context for the author's numerous Pushkin-related allusions:

> The first thing I learned about Pushkin was that he was killed. Then I learned that Pushkin was a poet and D'Anthès a Frenchman. D'Anthès hated Pushkin because he himself could not write poetry and challenged him to a duel—that is, he tricked him into coming out onto the snow, where he killed him with a gunshot in the stomach. This way, at the age of three, I learned for certain that poets have stomachs and—I am remembering all the poets I have ever met—this stomach of the poet, which is so often not full, and through which Pushkin was killed, worried me no less than his soul. I'll go further and say that there is something sacred for me in the word stomach: even a simple "My stomach hurts" covers me with a wave of shuddering sympathy that precludes any sort of humor. We were all wounded in the stomach with that shot. (translated by *M.G.*)

21. During Mikhail Gorbachev's "War on Alcoholism" in the late 1980s, grape arbors in Soviet Georgia were systematically chopped down.

22. Before the Russian revolution Joseph Stalin was arrested and exiled to Siberia.

23. In the early 17th century Russia was ruled by an impostor who became known as False Dmitri.

24. Nikolai Stepanovich Gumilyov (1886-1921), an Acmeist poet and the husband of Anna Akhmatova, was a White Guard officer executed by the Bolsheviks in August 1921.

25. Lenin once proffered the following definition: "Socialism equals Soviet rule plus the electrification of the entire country."

26. Poor Liza, the protagonist of Nikolai Karamzin's (an eighteenth-century Russian writer and historian) novel of the same name, commits suicide by drowning; Tatyana, or Tanya, the female protagonist of Pushkin's verse novel *Eugene Onegin,* marries an aging prince despite her love for Onegin himself; Tolstoy's Anna Karenina commits probably Russian literature's most famous suicide by throwing herself in front of an oncoming train.

27. A random listing of regions and forces dominant or significant at different times in Russian history.

28. Daylight savings time was re-introduced by Gorbachev during the perestroika period.

29. In the original Russian, the initials are N.Z., a loose allusion to Nikolai Zabolotsky (1903-1958), an poet who in the 1930s attempted to trade his experimental style for something more palatable to the state but was arrested in 1938 nonetheless; after returning to Moscow in 1946, he briefly achieved the status of a

poet approved by the state.

30. Mikhail Sergeyevich Gorbachev was named *Time* magazine's Man of the Year in 1987

31. A line from Goethe's *Faust.*

32. Beginning in the middle of the eighteenth century, members of the Russian nobility spoke French among themselves. The Duma was Russia's pre-revolutionary parliament.

33. The first line in this rhyming sequence is borrowed from Pushkin's *Eugene Onegin*

34. A reference to Soviet labor camps, where inmates were often used in timber production.

35. Some of Moscow's cathedrals are best remembered thanks to the film footage of their destruction by dynamite in the 1920s and 1930s.

36. The hill at the center of Moscow, on which Red Square and all the structures listed below are situated.

37. All the names in this paragraph are allusions to various Pushkin heroes from both his poems and prose.

ABOUT THE AUTHOR

Valeria Narbikova was born in Moscow in 1958. She graduated from the Gorky Literary Institute, and became one of the major writers of the post-Soviet period, publishing nine novels. In the early days of glasnost her work was labeled pornographic, despite its highly literary character, because Russian critics were simply not used to the idea that one could write casually and wittily about sex.

Her first novel, translated into English as *Day Equals Night,* won the *Iunost'* publication of the year award in 1989, and Narbikova was acclaimed as the voice of a previously mute generation. A hallmark of her style is the subversion of plot by means of digressions reminiscent of Laurence Sterne, as well as a tendency to mix all levels of language and all levels of allusion.

Narbikova's works have been translated into German, French, Italian, Japanese and English. Since 1980 Narbikova has also become known as a painter, and has had shows in America and Europe.

CF